"Garth, you're crushing me," Kate protested

"Mmm." He nuzzled against her neck and kept on sleeping.

"Garth, wake up. I can't breathe." Kate tried pushing at his chest, but he was like a rock. Finally she reached down and pinched his bottom.

With a yelp he rolled away from her, then regarded her with an injured expression. "Is that how you get rid of your lovers?"

Kate smiled and touched his cheek. "I was beginning to suffocate and you wouldn't wake up."

"Oh." His expression changed to chagrin. "Guess I was asleep. Not very romantic, huh?"

"But typical of many men, as I point out in my book. Research shows that most men fall asleep after sex. That's what causes some of the communication problems that women—"

"Whoa, Dr. Newberry." He grinned and caught her chin in his hand. "Let's talk about Garth and Kate. Did I insult you by falling asleep?"

She blushed. "No, because I understand it's a natural reaction to—"

"The best damn sex I've ever had!"

Vicki Lewis Thompson read a
fascinating article a few months ago about
one of the leading female "sexperts." Vicki
wondered what such experts are really
like—how do they cope with instant fame?
And how do they deal with an intimate
subject like sex day after day? Thus the
enticing plot behind *Ask Dr. Kate* was born.
Talented Vicki was recently honored by the
Romance Writers of America—*It Happened
One Weekend* was nominated for Best Short
Contemporary Novel of 1991.

Books by Vicki Lewis Thompson

HARLEQUIN TEMPTATION

240–BE MINE, VALENTINE
256–FULL COVERAGE
278–'TIS THE SEASON
288–FOREVER MINE, VALENTINE
344–YOUR PLACE OR MINE
374–IT HAPPENED ONE WEEKEND
396–ANYTHING GOES

HARLEQUIN SUPERROMANCE

326–SPARKS
389–CONNECTIONS
497–CRITICAL MOVES

ASK DR. KATE

VICKI LEWIS THOMPSON

Harlequin Books

TORONTO • NEW YORK • LONDON
AMSTERDAM • PARIS • SYDNEY • HAMBURG
STOCKHOLM • ATHENS • TOKYO • MILAN
MADRID • WARSAW • BUDAPEST • AUCKLAND

To Pat Warren,
who introduced me to the suite life

Published September 1992

ISBN 0-373-25510-1

ASK DR. KATE

Prologue

THE PHONE WAS RINGING as Kate walked in the door.

"Where have you been?" her agent demanded in her clipped New York accent when Kate answered the telephone.

"Counseling with a student down at the college. You told me not to quit my day job, Glenda."

"That advice may be outdated. Enthusiasm's building in-house for the book. They're considering a publicity tour. Marketing likes the way you photographed for the dust jacket, and they're trying to get you on Oprah or Donahue."

"Oprah or Donahue?" Kate laughed. "Come on, Glenda. I'm a psychologist, not a media personality."

"I tell you, they have plans. Plus, I told them you were promotable. Somebody's come up with 'Dr. Kate' as a gimmick." Glenda sounded nervous. "Isn't that a riot?"

Kate grimaced. "No. I'm up for a full professorship in the fall. Northbluff is a very conservative college. I don't think the committee will be impressed with a nickname like 'Dr. Kate.' Try to squash that idea."

"I'm not sure I can. It's . . . sort of on the back cover blurb."

"It's *printed* somewhere? Oh, Glenda. This is a work of scholarship. Can't you get the blurb changed?"

"Not now. The jackets are printed. And there's one other little thing." Glenda paused. "The title's been changed."

"The title? I already approved the title!"

"I know, but there was some mix-up in the art department. Marketing thought that *A Study of Female Repression* could be jazzed up somehow, and—"

"Jazzed up?"

"Well, somehow another title got printed instead of yours. It was a screwup, I'll admit," Glenda hurried on, her tone placating, "but supposedly the title is what has the marketing department all excited. They think they can really promote this book, especially with the red cover."

Kate groaned and closed her eyes. "What's the new title, Glenda?"

"Now don't prejudge. It's not so bad. Kind of catchy, in fact. You might even—"

"Just tell me what it is."

Glenda cleared her throat. "*Getting the Sex You Need from Your Man.*"

1

A DISPLAY OF IDENTICAL crimson hardcover volumes filled one window of the La Jolla Book Bag. Garth Fredericks glanced at them and sighed as he walked past on his way back to the Pelican Beach Resort. Just his luck that he'd chosen to fly in from Boston the very same week that this woman, some new self-help guru, was scheduled at the Pelican for a luncheon speech and autograph party.

Garth could easily imagine the type of bossy broad who would write something like *Getting the Sex You Need from Your Man*. She'd be as abrasive as his wife had become after reading a ton of similar books that eventually transformed her into his ex-wife. God, how he hated pop psychology.

What had happened to the simple formula of love, marriage and happily ever after? All this probing and dissecting of relationships just screwed things up as far as he was concerned. But most women he'd met recently were into all that stuff. No doubt Dr. Kate would pack them in.

He quickened his step along the boutique-and-restaurant-lined street leading toward the beach. The midday sun was making him start to sweat under his sport coat; he'd forgotten how hot California could be in October. Dr. Kate was due in about two, and it was nearly that now. He wanted to be safely back in his suite at the Pelican before the good doctor arrived.

Kate Newberry's presence brought welcome business to the resort, and as the owner Garth realized he ought to be pleased she was there. He knew that her book hadn't been out in time to contribute to the emotional and financial chaos of his divorce, but still, she was a member of the breed, and he didn't want to deal with her in person. His good buddy Boz could do that, assuming Boz was around.

Boz hadn't been in his office when Garth had left, which had been just as well. Garth had walked into town for lunch so he could think about the sorry mess Clyde Bosworth—Boz since their college days together—had made of managing this resort. Garth had thought he could do his old friend a favor by giving him the job, and for some reason Garth couldn't figure out, Boz had let the place go to hell. Maybe Boz had woman troubles. Garth could certainly understand that in this day and age. Or maybe Boz was afraid to admit he didn't know how to run a resort. Whatever the explanation, Garth hoped to find it soon.

The property was bordered by an eight-foot hedge of fuchsia oleanders that afford privacy from the road. Garth noted that they needed trimming. Beyond the hedge a lawn sloped sharply enough that only the Spanish tile roof of the resort's third story showed from the entrance road. And beyond the red-tiled roof sparkled the Pacific Ocean. It was a honey of a location.

When Garth had bought the property two years ago the lawn had been putting-green quality, the hedges clipped into neat rectangles, and the beach raked clean of seaweed daily. Boz's reign had changed all that. No guard was stationed at the security gate, either—another point to bring up when he and Boz had their inevitable talk, the one that might end with Garth firing his best friend. The fight with Judith and her lawyers had preoccupied Garth for the past year, and he hadn't kept tabs on the resort as he should have. He still might not have known how bad things were if he hadn't decided to fly out for some R and R.

With a sigh Garth started down the paved road toward the resort. Rounding the Pelican's circular driveway lined with unkempt beds of pink gardenias and violet petunias, he saw that he was too late to avoid the arrival of Dr. Kate. A black limousine stretched pantherlike beside the curb just beyond the resort's entrance and a uniformed driver helped a redhead in a white linen suit out of the back.

She had the lacquered, big-city look he'd expected, from her designer sunglasses to her stiletto heels. Her medium-length hair held a deceptively casual wave that probably required hours in a beauty salon. He imagined, although he couldn't tell from this distance, that she also sported a professional manicure with red nail polish and a perfectly applied mask of expensive cosmetics.

No one else emerged from the limo. He thought Boz had said something about a publicist accompanying her, but Dr. Kate appeared to be alone, although the chauffeur was unloading enough luggage for a family of four. Maybe the publicist would arrive separately.

Garth decided to linger in the driveway and wait until she and her myriad pieces of paisley luggage had been whisked into the hotel by someone on the bell staff. Timothy, the doorman, stood by expectantly. Timothy, Garth happened to know, liked celebrities. Garth usually found them to be a royal pain in the rear. In that respect he and Boz agreed. Unfortunately Boz's irreverence concerning celebrities had lost the resort some valuable business in the past year, judging from the stories Boz had recounted with great glee over a shared six-pack a few nights earlier.

Dr. Kate tipped the chauffeur and the sleek car pulled away from the curb. No bellman had arrived, and Dr. Kate looked impatient. Dammit, Garth thought, Boz must not have scheduled enough help for the day. In Garth's view the only thing worse than hosting someone of Dr. Kate's ilk was hosting her poorly. With another muttered oath he strode forward, seeing no choice but to handle the bags himself. Maybe he wouldn't have to reveal who he was.

As he passed the wide glass double doors to the lobby, he glanced in. The place was swarming with women and suitcases. Dr. Kate had drawn a big crowd of overnight guests, and Boz obviously hadn't planned ahead. This sort of sloppiness would eventually plunge the Pelican into the red. Garth couldn't afford that.

"Dr. Kate Newberry?" he asked, approaching her and the small mountain of luggage.

"Yes." She glanced at him suspiciously.

"The hotel seems to be a little short on bellmen today. I'll be glad to take these for you." He reached for the strap on her garment bag.

"Keep your hands off that." She moved forward, her lips set in a straight line.

"I was only—"

"No one touches my luggage except hotel personnel," she said. "I'm not about to be sucked into an arrangement wherein I'm obligated to some stranger who 'helps' with my bags and then, of course, has to know what room I'm in so he can deliver them."

"I'm with the hotel," Garth said, struggling to remain pleasant. Just as he'd suspected—she was hard as nails.

"If you're with the hotel, why are you in a jacket and tie? Where's your little uniform?" she asked.

Garth clenched his teeth and wondered if this was how she went about getting what she needed from men, sexually or otherwise. If so, he had to question her success rate. "We don't all wear uniforms."

"Then how am I supposed to believe that you're legitimate?"

Garth swallowed an instinctive, earthy response. "Please take my word for it. Now, if you'll allow me—" He reached for the garment bag again.

"I will not allow you a blessed thing." She grabbed the handle just as he did and tugged in the opposite direction. Timothy moved over behind her, as if to help in some way, and then stood there, apparently wondering what was correct protocol.

Garth didn't relinquish his hold. At such close range he was surrounded by the lemon fragrance of her cologne, and without really trying he could see the shadow of her cleavage as she leaned over to grasp the bag and the vee of her pink blouse gaped a little. Okay, so she wasn't completely without sex appeal. So the white linen skirt displayed a slim waist and nice hips. He reminded himself who she was and what she'd written.

Narrowing his eyes, he tried to pierce the barrier of her dark glasses. "Dr. Newberry, I would appreciate it if you'd allow me to take your luggage to your room," he said evenly. "We seem to have a shortage of bellmen this afternoon and I would be *honored* to take care of you personally." He laid on the charm with a trowel, amazing himself. Boz owed him big-time for this.

"I'll just bet you would like to take care of me 'personally.'" Her warm breath, mint scented, touched his face.

An image of kissing her startled the hell out of him. He pushed it away. "I'm only offering to carry your luggage, Dr. Newberry," he said.

"You don't fool me for a minute. You're like all the other men I've met recently." She tugged harder on the garment bag. "You want Dr. Kate as the latest notch on your belt."

That did it. The insult was unfair, considering that his intentions had been completely honorable, even if his thoughts hadn't been completely chaste. "As you like," he said, releasing the handle and throwing her slightly off balance. She stumbled against Timothy, who set her upright and glanced at Garth for some sign as to what he was supposed to do next.

Garth shrugged. Aside from throwing this uppity woman over his shoulder and grabbing a suitcase in each hand, he was out of ideas. An airport van approached the hotel, no doubt bringing more of Dr. Kate's loyal fans. Maybe they'd like to carry her luggage.

"Just where *are* the bellmen?" she demanded, putting her hands on her hips.

"Oh, probably off somewhere cutting notches in their belts. You know how men are, especially in California," Garth said, unable to help himself. He was angry at her, angrier still at himself for reacting to her sexually. But thoughts weren't actions, he rationalized, and he wasn't into belt notches. "Now if you'll excuse me, I have work to do."

"Wait."

He wanted to ignore her command, but he was, after all, a gentleman. He paused.

"Just exactly who are you?"

"Garth Fredericks. Owner of the hotel."

"A likely story."

Timothy, the doorman, spoke up. "He is, Dr. Newberry. He's flown in from back East."

Color tinged her cheeks, but to her credit she maintained her composure. "You should have said so in the first place."

"Believe me, I wish I had."

"I, uh, would appreciate your help with these bags."

Without another word he shouldered the strap to her garment bag, tucked a second suitcase under his arm and clutched the handles of the two smaller pieces in his other hand. It was a heavy load. "Your fans are waiting for you in the lobby," he said, starting toward the door Timothy held open. He would not stagger, he vowed.

"Oh, please, is there another way in?"

He stopped, surprised. He'd figured her for someone who loved the spotlight. "There's a service entrance. We can handle check in without going through the registration desk, if that's what you want."

"I would be eternally grateful."

He thought of the longer walk to the kitchen door, and the weight of the suitcases. He should have grabbed a luggage cart before attempting this insanity, but he hated to admit that now. "Then follow me," he said. As he lugged everything around to the side of the building, he wondered if she'd filled the suitcases with copies of her books.

She followed him, her high heels tapping decisively on the brick walkway that led to the kitchen. He'd expected a firm stride from a woman who'd written something with a title as brazen as *Getting the Sex You Need from Your Man*. At the service entrance he put down two of the suitcases with a little sigh of relief and pressed the buzzer for someone to open the door.

"Are there staffing problems at this hotel?" she asked as they waited.

Among other things, Garth thought. "Not normally," he said. "We may have underestimated the number of guests your appearance here would bring."

"I hope there'll be no trouble tomorrow. We have to have waiters and busboys and all those kinds of people."

"We will have those kinds of people," Garth promised grimly as the door was finally opened by a young kid in a white apron. The kid didn't even look surprised, just went back to sweeping the floor as Garth ushered his charge inside and picked up his burden once more. He led Kate through the steamy kitchen to the service elevator, where he was able, once again, to unload some of the weight he was carrying.

They rode in silence to the third floor and the elevator filled with the citrusy scent of her cologne. Garth tried to ignore it. Fortunately he remembered which suite Boz had set up for her. It was a corner unit facing the ocean, with a balcony, a king-size bed, and a sitting room. Both the bedroom and sitting room had sliding glass doors that opened onto the balcony. Garth knew the room well because his was exactly like it, one floor below. He and Boz had joked about the logistics. From the title of her book they both figured that this was a woman who'd like being on top.

Thinking of that, Garth forgave himself for his earlier sexual thoughts about her. A book like hers invited men to think about sex when they were around her. She could hardly blame the nature of men or complain that they all wanted notches in their belts. She was the one who'd brought up the subject.

Garth glanced over at her. She'd taken off her dark glasses and was twirling them in one hand. Her brown eyes were shadowed with fatigue, and she leaned against the side of the elevator, as if she couldn't stand erect another second. Yet there was a nervous energy in her movement with the glasses, and Garth noted the tense line of her mouth and the convulsive swallow that undulated the gentle curve of her throat. He'd been wrong about the polish on her fingernails. It was pink, not red.

For a moment the combative woman he'd wrestled for possession of her luggage seemed different, more vulnerable. Then she caught him looking at her. She straightened and tucked her glasses into an outside pocket of her leather shoulder bag. Her chin went up, as if she dared him to make a comment about her lapse into human frailty. Garth glanced away again.

When the door opened he checked the hallway. "The coast is clear," he said, and led her toward her suite.

"Until someone finds out where I'm staying," she said, "or bribes the switchboard to put unauthorized calls through."

"We don't give out room numbers," Garth said, hoping to hell that was still true. "And the switchboard has your list of authorized callers," he added.

"I've heard that six times, in six different cities, and someone always gets through, anyway."

He used his master key in the lock and stood back to let her go in first. "How many days have you been on this tour?" he asked, aware that he was probably being unwise to attempt any sort of conversation.

"Ten." Not even bothering to look at the ocean view beyond the balcony's wrought-iron railing, she sank down on a flowered love seat.

"Ten." Normally he would have left the door ajar when he was in the room with a guest, but this time for security reasons he closed it with one foot. Six cities in ten days. No wonder she looked so tired. But her weariness wasn't his business, he told himself. Besides, she'd brought it on herself, by writing a book that begged for that kind of promotion.

He didn't blame her publishers for sending her on a speaking tour and raking in the dough while they could. He'd have done the same thing if he'd been in charge. In a year she'd be old news. But six cities in ten days was a punishing pace. "Is your publicist coming in later?" he asked, remembering Boz had reserved an adjoining room in addition to the suite.

"No. She had a family emergency come up this morning. We decided, since this was the last stop on the tour, that I could manage. So I hope the hotel has everything in place for tomorrow, Mr. Fredericks, because I don't have Stella to run interference for me."

"Don't worry about a thing." Garth cursed inwardly. The publicist might have kept Boz on his toes. Now Garth would probably have to do it. "I'll put your bags in here," he said, moving into the adjacent bedroom.

"Fine. Thanks," she added, as if prompting herself to be polite.

Garth tried to remember what a bellman was supposed to do. "Would you like anything unpacked or pressed?"

"No. No, thanks," she said, as if every interchange was an effort. He had the impression she'd like him out of there so she could get out of her restrictive business clothes and into the large Roman tub in the bathroom. A brief image of that stirred an amazingly quick response in him. He reminded himself that he didn't like anything about her type. Well, maybe her cologne. Maybe the thought of her body without all that paraphernalia. Definitely not her choice of profession.

He walked back into the sitting room and discovered, as he'd expected, that she was exactly where he'd left her, her back straight, her eyes slightly unfocused, her mind apparently in an exhaustion-induced trance.

She snapped to awareness as he entered the room. "I've never had my luggage transported by an owner of the hotel before," she said, reaching for the clasp on her purse. "Should I tip you?"

"Not on your life." He backed away and managed a smile. "Have a nice evening."

"Yes. Thank you."

He was almost to the door when the phone beside the love seat rang. He heard her pick it up as he turned the doorknob. He was nearly out the door when she started screaming into the receiver.

"Slimeball!" she cried. "You sneaky, scummy excuse for a man!" She slammed the receiver into the cradle.

Garth paused. He should leave. Probably some fight with her boyfriend. Maybe her man had failed to give her the sex she needed. Garth started out the door again.

"That's it. Just slink away, pretend you have no responsibility," she said.

He tensed. Slowly he faced her. "Excuse me?"

She stood glaring at him, her hands on her hips. "I suppose you'll give me some cock-and-bull story about how there's nothing you can do. That's what they all say."

He flexed his fingers and met her belligerence with a steady gaze. "That depends on what you want done."

"I want my privacy guarded. I've been in this room five minutes and it's already been violated."

"That wasn't one of your authorized callers?"

She laughed bitterly. "No, that wasn't one of my authorized callers. And it seems he's found me. Again."

That wasn't quite fair, and she knew it.
She felt their pity. Kate didn't want one bit of anyone's pity. And it wasn't a found one either.

2

"WHO'S FOUND YOU?" Garth asked. "What do you mean?"

Kate studied the man in front of her and wondered if there was any point in going into it. The police in Denver had said the guy could be very hard to catch. But Garth Fredericks had a commanding attitude that appealed to her. He seemed the type who wouldn't take guff from anyone. Maybe he *would* help her. "I don't know who he is," she began, "but he latched on to me in Houston, the fourth city of my tour, and started calling my hotel room. I thought I'd be rid of him once I left Houston, but he followed me to Denver and made phone calls to my room there. He's never approached me in person, or at least I don't think he has. Only these telephone calls."

"How do you know he's followed you? Couldn't they be long-distance calls?"

Kate shook her head. "He always mentions what I wore that day, and how he'd—well, never mind."

"The calls are obscene."

"Very."

"And he's followed you all the way from Texas. Sounds more persistent than your average creep."

Kate looked into his gray eyes and saw that he was taking her seriously. She appreciated that. "He does have me worried," she admitted. "Especially after this last call. He said he'd be seeing me soon."

"He's never said that before?"

"No. Maybe he's moving in because this is the last personal appearance on the tour. He obviously got my itinerary from someone, which wouldn't have been hard. After all, the publisher wants everyone to know where I'll be appearing."

"What about your publicist—Stella, was it? What does she think?"

"She was concerned and had notified the publisher, but then this morning she got word that her father had a massive heart attack. I guess we both forgot about this guy in the frenzy to find her a plane ride home. I didn't think of him, quite frankly, until you offered to carry my luggage."

The look in his eyes softened. "So that's why you snarled at me."

"I didn't snarl. I was protecting myself. Would a man let some stranger grab his suitcases? But let a woman protest because someone wants to take charge of her life, and everyone—"

"All right, all right." Garth held up one hand.

"You have no idea what it's like." Once started, Kate wouldn't be stopped by some stupid hand signal. "I've been put on display like a circus animal, treated like this *commodity*. People think they can say anything they want, do anything that comes to mind, as if I don't have feelings, as if—" She realized Garth was staring at her, and that she was dangerously close to tears. She turned away.

"You're right, I have no idea what it's like to be a celebrity." His voice relayed quiet strength. "I can't protect you from that part of it, but I can damn sure do something about this jerk who's hounding you. Nobody should have to go through that kind of harassment."

Kate took a long breath and felt some of her tension ease. She turned back to him. "Thank you." For the first time since the heckler had called in Houston, she felt that someone could help. She hadn't started out very well with Garth, but who could blame her for being suspicious? When he'd offered to carry her luggage, her first thought, understandably, had been that he was the man on her trail. Now that she knew he wasn't, she could relax and see him as a potential ally.

She'd hardly noticed before how physically appealing he was. He had a straight nose and his chin had a small cleft in it. His hair was thick and wavy—dark brown except for a faint sprinkling of gray at the temples. Frown lines between his brows told her he'd had his share of problems, too, but she didn't miss the laugh lines around his mouth, or the sensuous fullness of his lower lip. She judged him to be in his late thirties and noticed he wore no wedding band. He wasn't a tall man, perhaps only about five-ten to her five-six, but he had a good build and carried himself well. His carriage, as well as the way he'd stood up to her when she wouldn't let him take her bags, had given her the feeling that he'd be a formidable opponent. She could use a man like that on her side.

"I think you should trade suites with me," Garth said. "I'm in the one directly below you, so the setup is the same. We won't tell the switchboard, in case your guy has made a contact with somebody there. I can field all your messages and you can do the same for me. That might eliminate the phone calls."

Kate considered the suggestion. "Won't people think I have a man living in my room?"

"So what? Considering the book you're promoting, that fits right in with your image."

She recoiled as if slapped. "It most certainly does not!" To think she'd nearly transformed him into her knight in shining armor, and he was like all the rest.

"Come on, Dr. Newberry. You said yourself that most of the men you meet want you as a belt notch. I agree you don't deserve someone like this sicko hanging around, but books like you've written, advertising that you want sex practically on demand, are bound to make most people think—"

"I do not advocate sex on demand," she said, longing to wipe the patronizing expression off his face. "And I want you out of my room. Now."

"Under the circumstances, that's a dangerous attitude to take."

She advanced toward him. "I'll be the judge of that. The point is, I don't want your help, or your precious room. I'll deal with this creep myself, rather than listen to your insinuations about my personal life."

His gray eyes glinted with resolve. "You may not want my help, but you'll get it. You're a guest in my hotel, and I have to take whatever measures I deem necessary to keep you safe. If you won't abide by that, then you're free to go elsewhere and reschedule your luncheon. It's up to you."

How she longed to leave this hotel, leave it and fly somewhere remote, like the Australian outback, where they'd never heard of Dr. Kate or her book about sex. Garth's comment wasn't unique. Other men had accused her of the same sort of thing since the book came out. It was her fault, for not pitching a royal fit and making them change the title, no matter what it cost in reprinted book jackets. But she had reluctantly agreed to the title, and the publicity tour, and the make-over, and the talk show in L.A. next week. She'd agreed out of inexperience and a desire to see her words in print, read by thousands of people. She wondered how many of those thousands had read only the title.

If she canceled this luncheon and disappeared, the publishers might be able to sue her for loss of revenue, not to mention what would happen to her academic career at Northbluff College. She'd already heard the committee was reconsidering whether to grant her a full professorship. If she ran away from her obligations the college might decide to fire such an untrustworthy member of its faculty. Both Stella and Glenda had said that was okay, she could get a job anywhere now. But she wanted the job she had, on a small campus in Nebraska, where life progressed at a slow and predictable pace. She wanted her old life back.

As she stood there, wondering if there was any way out of the mess she was in, the telephone rang. She glanced at it and then looked at Garth. He lifted an eyebrow as the telephone pealed again. Finally he walked past her and picked up the receiver.

His voice was low and menacing as he said "Yeah?" Then he slowly replaced the receiver and turned around. "Funny, but he didn't want to talk to me."

Fear churned in her stomach. She'd tried so hard to be brave about this, and the situation made her mad as hell, but she was afraid, too. The man seemed to become more aggressive with each phone call, and as a psychologist she knew what that meant. Eventually he'd work himself up to some sort of physically threatening act.

"Ready to trade rooms?" Garth asked.

She hesitated for only a moment more before nodding her assent. One night. She only had to get through one more night and her life would be her own again. At least she had to believe that. She'd be better off in Garth's suite. His opinion of her and her book made no real difference.

"We'll take the fire stairs," Garth said, going back into the bedroom to retrieve her suitcases. "Wait here until I see if anyone's in the hall."

"I'm carrying some of those suitcases." Kate didn't want to be any more obligated to him than necessary.

"Not in my hotel you're not," he said, coming out of the bedroom laden down like a pack animal.

"That's stupid. You have far too much pride for your own good. You—" She stopped herself, knowing she was only trying to retaliate. She should be used to his attitude; she'd been encountering similar attitudes ever since the book hit the stands two weeks ago.

His gray gaze swept over her. "You're not the first woman to accuse me of having too much pride, and you probably won't be the last." Then he headed for the door.

That was how she should have handled his comments about her book and her sex life, she thought. She should have told him that she was used to such opinions by now, in that same world-weary tone he'd just used. She'd work on that.

She followed him to the door, but he motioned her back until he'd checked the hall. Finally he ushered her out ahead of him and pointed her toward the fire stairs. As he closed the door to her suite, the phone started ringing again.

Inside the well of the fire stairs their footsteps echoed as they walked down a floor.

"This isn't very stealthy," Kate said, her voice echoing, too.

"I didn't claim to have the skills of a cat burglar," Garth said as the suitcases banged off the narrow walls of the stairway. "If you have a better suggestion, let's hear it."

"No, I don't. I don't think in those terms. Never had to before. I've never had to hide from anyone in my life."

"Shouldn't have written the book," Garth muttered.

"Look, could you just stuff—" Kate caught herself and took a deep breath. "Many people have told me that," she said, sounding bored. "You're certainly not the first."

Her statement was met with silence, and then she thought she heard a snort of muffled laughter. But perhaps she was wrong. It could have been one of her suitcases brushing against the stairwell.

He didn't speak again until they reached the second floor. "Open the door just a little and check the hall," he instructed her. "Then go straight to the same room we were in on the third floor." He set down two of the suitcases and reached in his pants' pocket. "And take the key."

She did, careful not to touch his hand in the process. She wanted no physical contact with a man who thought she advocated sex on demand, a man who hadn't taken the time to read her book before judging it and her. She knew he hadn't read it; by now she could tell by the way people talked to her whether they'd bothered to go beyond the jacket copy.

The hall was empty and she hurried over to the door of his suite. She was inside in no time, with Garth right behind her. He closed the door with his shoulder and headed into the bedroom with her luggage.

"I'll pack up my stuff. Shouldn't take long," he said over his shoulder.

"Fine." She wandered around the sitting room while she listened to him open closets and drawers. From the sound of it he wasn't taking much care. No doubt he wanted out of here as much as she wanted him out.

As he'd said, the suite was identical to the one she'd originally had, but there was a subtle difference. He'd been living here and the scent of his shaving cream and lotion hung in the air. The sliding door to the balcony stood open, and the salty breeze drifted in, riffling the pages of an investment magazine on the coffee table in front of the love seat.

Other signs of his presence were scattered around the room: a pair of gold cuff links on an end table, along with a pad of notepaper with some figures jotted down in a firm, bold hand. A burgundy leather briefcase, monogrammed, sat beside a chair covered in the same flowered pattern as the love seat, and a television guide folded back to the current date was on top of the video cabinet next to an economy-size jar of peanuts. She was amused that someone who owned a hotel had brought his own peanuts rather than eat the snacks in the courtesy bar.

She'd started out through the sliding door to inspect the view of the ocean when he came into the room with his garment bag slung over his shoulder. "I wouldn't go out there if I were you," he said.

She stopped. Of course she shouldn't go out there. "I didn't think," she said, knowing that incredible as it seemed, she had forgotten for that brief moment about the man after her. The sound of Garth rummaging around in the other room and her inventory of his belongings in the sitting room had given her a feeling of safety.

"Well, you have to keep thinking." He picked up the cuff links and shoved them into his coat pocket. "Hang the Do Not Disturb sign on the knob and leave it there until you check out tomorrow, and I'll do the same. That way the maids don't have to know about this, either."

"Good idea."

"If anyone calls your room while I'm there, I'll take a message. I'd appreciate you taking my messages, too." He reached for his briefcase.

"I know you're not worried about my reputation, but what about yours?" she asked. "For all I know, you have a girlfriend who might be calling here."

"I have an ex-wife," he said. "Dealing with her hasn't left me much time for girlfriends, so don't worry about it. And Judith won't be calling. Boz—he's the manager of the Pelican—has promised me that the switchboard won't put her calls through."

"I take it you didn't have an amicable divorce?" Kate wondered if Judith was responsible for some of the frown lines on Garth's brow.

Raising both eyebrows, he glanced at her. "Now why would you want to know that, Dr. Kate? Trying to get a psychological bead on me, by any chance?"

"That's unfair! Your statement about your ex-wife implied that you don't get along with her. I was only making an observation. And don't use that nickname in my presence, Mr. Fredericks."

"In your presence? It's plastered all over the place!"

"I had nothing to do with that."

"Oh, I see. You're an innocent bystander in all this. Fame and fortune was the last thing you expected when you wrote that book."

"That's right."

He laughed. "Sure," he said, grabbing his briefcase.

She opened her mouth to argue and realized she was rising to the bait yet again. For some reason this man wanted a fight, and she was obligingly giving it to him. "Thank you for the use of your suite," she said.

He regarded her pensively. "You're welcome. And speaking of ex-wives and significant others, do you have some bone-crusher of a jealous boyfriend who'll fly down and pulverize me if a man answers your phone?"

Kate wished she could say she did. Then maybe Garth wouldn't think she was some free-wheeling sex maniac. But Danforth was long gone. In her most vindictive moments she blamed him for this entire debacle. If he hadn't psychologically kicked her in the teeth, she'd never have written her book.

"No boyfriend," she said. "The only people on my authorized caller list are my editor, my agent, my mother, and a colleague at the school where I teach. All of them are female, and all of them would probably be delighted at the novelty of hearing a male voice answer my telephone." She'd thrown in the last statement purely for effect. For some stupid reason, she didn't want him to think of her as promiscuous. And she'd accused *him* of having too much pride.

"Okay," he said slowly, apparently digesting the information.

She thought there was a different light in his eyes, as if he was reevaluating her, but perhaps that was wishful thinking on her part. Why did she care, anyway? "Don't forget your magazine," she said, glancing at the coffee table.

"I've read it. If you're interested, you're welcome to it. Maybe you'll need some of that information when the royalties start rolling in."

"Maybe." She gazed at him. "We could trade reading material," she said slowly, knowing she was asking for it, but hoping that perhaps, just perhaps . . .

He obviously knew what she was suggesting. He shook his head. "Sorry, but that's the last thing in the world I'd read."

Damn, she thought, glancing away. No matter how thick-skinned she tried to be, she never quite succeeded in handling rejection. "Then I don't know how you have the gall to lecture me about whether I should have written it. You don't even know what it's about."

"Oh, yes, I do."

"Just because of the title?"

"Because of everything—the title, the hype, the section where it's shelved in the bookstore."

"That's not the least bit open-minded. You're not giving the book a chance."

"That's right. I'm not," he said, and walked out the door.

She waited until he closed it. Then she picked up his magazine and hurled it across the room. "You arrogant bastard!" she cried. Then she noticed that he'd left something behind. The jar of peanuts was still on top of the television cabinet. Well, too bad for him. She happened to like peanuts. He would just have to eat the expensive snacks in the courtesy bar in her room. Crossing to the cabinet, she unscrewed the lid of the jar and poured several peanuts into her hand. It felt good to have something to crunch on. She ate the peanuts with a satisfying sense of revenge.

An hour later she'd stripped to her underwear and was unpacked—as much as she'd planned to unpack for a one-night stay. The bathroom still smelled of Garth's after-shave, so she sprayed some of her perfume in the air, creating a mix of his spicy scent and her citrusy one. The combination disturbed her; the mingled fragrances taunted her with an intimacy that didn't exist and never would. For which she was certainly glad. Certainly was.

Kate groaned. For all her training in human psychology, life sometimes tripped her up, and this was one of those times. In spite of his arrogance, his close-minded refusal to read her book, and his unfounded suspicions about her personal habits, Garth Fredericks was the most attractive man she'd met in many long months, and she was drawn to him. God help her, maybe he represented a challenge.

As she put her cosmetics in the bathroom, she thought of him standing at the same sink, his hips wrapped in a towel, while he shaved that morning. She wondered if he had much hair on his chest. She'd guess from the thickness of the hair on his head that he did. Then she wondered if he shaved wrapped in a towel at all.

Thoughts of Garth made her restless. She discarded the idea of a shower, because the shower was more masculine, his domain. She could picture him behind the pebbled glass, water sluicing over his muscled body as he rubbed a bar of soap over his chest and arms, across his taut belly, down.... She had to get a grip on herself.

She'd use the Roman tub. She couldn't picture Garth lying back against the curve of porcelain, soaking in the warm water as she planned to do. Except perhaps when he had a woman to share the bathing experience with. But she remembered him saying he'd had no girlfriends since he was divorced. That didn't mean no women, though, just no girlfriends. There was a difference. The difference seemed even more evocative. She couldn't imagine him as celibate, only wary of entanglements. He wouldn't confirm her comment about his ex-wife, but he looked like a man who'd been burned and had vowed to stay away from the flame.

But then, she was suspicious of men, too. Danforth had been so slick at winning her love and trust that she'd reacted in disbelief to the evidence that he was conducting a simultaneous affair with a housewife in a nearby town. His carefully hidden contempt for women had caught her by surprise and shook her self-confidence. After all, she was supposed to understand human motivation. That was her job.

Her experience with Danforth had made her wary of developing a new relationship. One-night stands weren't her style, nor did they fit in with the life of a female professor in a small midwestern college town, so she'd remained celibate. Perhaps too damned celibate, judging from her elemental reaction to Garth Fredericks.

It was probably her exhaustion, she thought as she ran herself a tub and added bubble bath. Exhaustion and vulnerability had endowed Garth with more allure than he really possessed. If she'd met him before the book had sold, when she'd felt safe, she might have been more amused by his macho behavior. But today, when he'd taken on her security problem and practically forced her to do things his way, not only had she been grateful and impressed, she'd felt a thrill of sexual excitement.

The warm bath made her less restless, but more aware of her body, and what she'd been missing ever since Danforth had taken himself out of her life and her bed.

She sank into the tub up to her chin, closed her eyes and tried to make her mind a blank. Pictures of Garth kept intruding—not Garth as she'd seen him in his suit, issuing orders, but Garth as she wished he would be, 'seducing her with a touch, a look, a whispered word. This Garth wouldn't view her book or her with disdain. This Garth would know how to arouse her, how to bring out the temptress in her that Danforth had nearly eradicated.

Lost in her fantasy, she almost didn't hear the knock at the door to the suite. She bolted out of the water and grabbed a terry-cloth robe provided by the hotel. As she put it on she realized that Garth must have used it, too. The scent of his after-shave swirled upward, as if he were enclosing her in his arms. Had he come back? Had he somehow sensed her response to him? Had he returned to apologize, to say, of course he'd read her book, of course he'd like to get to know her better?

Her heart pounding, her feet making damp prints across the cream-colored carpet, she approached the door and peered through the peephole. The man on the other side was not Garth.

The peephole distorted the man's image so that his head seemed larger than his body, but she could still tell that he was muscular and blond, and she'd never seen him before in her life.

Kate's mouth went dry. *I'll see you soon, bitch.* Her caller's low, hoarse voice seemed to echo in the room with her. She didn't know his methods for finding her, but he seemed to be good at it. She was safe, though. The door had a dead bolt. As long as she didn't open the door, he couldn't get her. She'd call Garth. While the man stood outside her door, she'd call Garth, very quietly, and tell him to send the police.

Keeping her eye on the door, Kate edged back toward the telephone next to the love seat. The man pounded on the door again. He sounded impatient. Of course he was impatient. He'd waited since Houston for this chance. Kate picked up the receiver.

The number of Garth's room—what was it? What was the damned room number? How did she dial another room? *Focus, Newberry!* A new sound at the door. A key inserted in the lock. He had a key!

Fast. She had to do something fast. Dropping the receiver she ran across the room and grabbed the peanut jar. Then she dashed behind the door so that it would hide her as it opened. And it did open. The key was the right one.

Kate clenched the jar. Her hands were slippery with sweat but she couldn't miss. Her heart pounded so loud in her ears she couldn't hear the man's footsteps as he came through the door. He almost squashed her as he threw it open. She eased herself out, not breathing. Slowly she raised the jar, her gaze fixed on a spot at the back of his head. She had to get it right the first time. She'd have no other chance.

Whack! She swung the jar and it connected with a sickening crunch that broke the glass. Peanuts scattered everywhere. The man staggered, made a surprised little sound, and crumpled to the floor.

Kate almost crumpled with him. She'd done it! Her breath came out in great heaving gasps. The man groaned, and she realized that he might not be unconscious for long. She'd have to tie him up. She dropped to her knees, trying to avoid any pieces of broken glass.

Whipping off the tie from her robe, she picked up one beefy wrist and brought it behind his back. A square knot. Left and under. Right and under. When his wrists were roped together, she had some of the tie left over. She added his feet to the same bundle. He looked like a calf at a rodeo, but he was immobilized and still unconscious, although he'd groaned a couple of times.

Kate stood up unsteadily and pulled her robe together. Now she could call Garth. She stepped around peanuts and broken glass and walked to the phone. Some help he'd been. She wondered how this man had worked so quickly. To find out that she'd switched to his room and to have obtained a key in the space of two hours showed that he had inside contacts. Nobody except Garth was even supposed to know that she was in this room. Garth must have let the information slip, the jerk, and she'd almost paid the price. Garth was some hero, all right.

At least the nightmare would be over, now. She picked up the telephone receiver and dialed the front desk. Not much use for secrecy anymore. She had to clear her throat before she could speak. "Could you find Garth Fredericks at once and tell him to come immediately to Room 234?" The desk clerk sounded confused. "Yes, I know that is—was—his room. Just get him."

After she hung up the phone she glanced at the hogtied man and the open door. Perhaps she should close it, in case someone happened along. No use in calling attention to this matter. Maybe she could persuade the police to be discreet. The press would get wind of this somehow, she had no doubt, but the longer she could delay the reports, the better. Skirting the peanuts and glass, she pushed the door nearly closed.

She started picking up peanuts and chunks of the jar, and the man moaned again. A purple lump was growing on the back of his head. She paused and wondered if she ought to have something to hit him with again, in case he came to before Garth arrived. Throwing the glass and peanuts into a nearby wastebasket, she returned to her bedroom and came out with one of her books. She always had twenty copies with her in case she ever got to an autographing before the books did.

She sat on the love seat with her book and kept watch over the inert man. She stayed there for what seemed like hours until a tap came at the door and Garth's voice, sounding worried, called out, "Kate?"

She noted the use of her first name and that he sounded very concerned. Good. Of course, she'd taken care of everything and his concern wasn't worth much at this point. She savored the thought of his impending humiliation as he realized how inadequate he was and how resourceful she'd been. "Come in, Garth," she said. "I've caught the stalker."

"What?" He flung open the door. He'd discarded his suit jacket and tie, and his shirtsleeves were rolled up. He stared at the man on the floor. "Oh, my God."

"He knew where I was. He had a key to the room. I knocked him out," she said in a satisfied tone.

"My God," Garth said again, and dropped to his knees beside the man. He began untying Kate's careful square knots.

"What are you doing?" she asked, rushing forward and stepping on a piece of glass in the process.

"This isn't your stalker," Garth said, working furiously at the knots. "You've knocked out my manager, Clyde Bosworth."

3

"YOUR MANAGER?" Kate gasped.

"Also my best friend." Garth pulled the terry-cloth belt free, releasing Boz's arms and legs. "Call 911." Garth leaned down and peered into Boz's face. "Hey, buddy," he murmured. "You'll be fine. Help's on the way." He wished he knew more about first aid. The lump on the back of Boz's head was purple and growing. It was already the size of a golf ball.

Kate hung up the phone. "The paramedics are on the way," she said, sounding scared. "Garth, I didn't mean to—when he came right in I thought he was the man who's been—"

"I know." Garth didn't look up. He concentrated on Boz's breathing, which seemed okay. "Get some ice, will you?"

"Yes. Ice. Where's the machine?"

"Down the hall to your right," he said. Then he remembered that she wasn't supposed to be wandering around out there, drawing attention to herself. He glanced up and saw she was halfway to the door, heedless of her own safety, clad only in a terry robe that she was clutching around herself because she'd used the belt to tie up Boz. "Wait," he called. "You can't go. I'll go. Watch him."

She turned, her expression open and vulnerable. "Okay."

He got to his feet. "Close the door and don't let anyone in except me or the paramedics."

"I won't."

He held her gaze for a moment longer. Pushing through his worry about Boz was a growing awareness of her—her face scrubbed clean of makeup, her hair slightly damp, her body naked under the robe. Impatient with himself, he shook his head. Here she'd just decked his best buddy in the world and he was having lusty thoughts about her. When he glanced away, he noticed spots of blood on the cream-colored carpet. "Who's bleeding?"

"Me, I guess." She turned up one foot to reveal a smear of blood. "I stepped on a piece of glass."

He felt the sharp sting in his own flesh. "Take care of it," he said, more roughly than he'd meant to.

"I'll pay for cleaning the rug," she said quickly. "I'll pay for any medical bills for your friend, too," she added.

"I don't care about that!" He realized when she blanched that she thought he was angry with her. "Listen, it's okay. Everything will be okay," he said more softly. "I'll be back in a minute. Lock the door after me." He made his way through the glass and peanuts and hurried out the door. He had to get away from the inappropriate urges she was generating in him. This was not the same Kate Newberry he'd battled earlier in the day, and the transformation was bringing back all the erotic images that her first appearance had stirred up in him—images he'd tried to banish from his mind. A brusque businesswoman who wrote *Getting the Sex You Need from Your Man* was one thing; a half-clothed nymph straight out of a bubble bath was quite another.

He returned with the ice and rapped on the door. "It's me," he called, and the door swung open.

She'd retrieved the tie to her robe and had a tissue held against the ball of her foot with a rubber band.

"Ingenious," he said, glancing at her foot.

"It was all I could find," she said, limping toward Boz.

Garth noticed that the tie wasn't doing a complete job of keeping the robe closed. But simply knowing that she had nothing on under the robe would have sent his imagination whirling, regardless. He recognized the robe as the same one he'd used that morning. Now it was enclosing her body, nestling against her skin. . . .

"He's waking up," she said, nodding toward Boz.

Garth glanced down at his friend, who moaned and started to push himself to his knees. "Don't move, buddy," Garth said, crossing to him and crouching down. "The paramedics will be here any minute."

"What the hell happened?" Boz said, his voice thick. "I come in to leave you a note, and next thing I see is stars."

"A misunderstanding," Garth said.

"I don't think I've ever felt this misunderstood. My head aches like a son of a bitch. What hit me?"

"I'll explain in a minute," Garth said, putting down the ice bucket and helping Boz ease back to a prone position. "I'm going to fix some ice."

Boz groaned as he laid his head back on the carpet. "Could you pour about two fingers of Scotch over it?"

"Not yet. Stay still."

When Garth returned with ice wrapped in a wash-cloth, he found Kate on her hands and knees picking up shards of glass and tossing them in a wastebasket while she apologized profusely to Boz.

"I explained to him that it was all my fault," she said, glancing up. "I really feel awful about this, Garth."

"I don't know how you can take the rap. Blame that bozo who's on your trail, if you want to blame anyone." Garth knelt in a cleared space and gently laid the ice against the purple lump. Boz yelled. "Easy," Garth said. "I think this is good for you."

"You *think?*" Boz protested. "For this kind of torture, you sure as hell better *know* it's good for me."

"It's good for you," Kate said gently. "It will keep the swelling down until the paramedics arrive."

Garth glanced across at her as she continued to pick up glass. Beneath the terry cloth her breasts swayed as she moved, and he stared hungrily. The sound of her voice just now, coupled with the potential availability of her body under the robe, combined to form one of the most powerful attractions to a woman he'd ever felt in his life. He wanted to hear that soothing, caring voice again, speaking to him instead of Boz. He wanted to un-tie her robe and caress her until they were both senseless with desire. Hadn't her book proclaimed that she needed sex? Well, he was the man to give it to her.

Boz groaned again. "Don't press so damned hard, buddy," he complained.

Garth jerked back to reality and almost dropped the washcloth full of ice. "Sorry," he mumbled, chastising himself for being a fool, a fantasizing fool. What on God's green earth had he been thinking of, with his friend lying here in pain? "Forget the rest of the glass," he said, wanting her to move away, to stop crawling around on the carpet with her unfettered breasts exactly at his eye level. "The maid will vacuum."

"I thought we didn't want a maid in here?" she asked.

Garth sighed. "You're right. But stop for now, okay? You'd better put some clothes on before the paramedics get here."

She looked at him for a long moment, her brown gaze seeming to assess him. "I suppose so," she said, and left the room. The bedroom door closed.

Boz made a sound halfway between a laugh and a snort. "Spoilsport."

"You dirty old man," Garth said, discovering to his amazement that he really was irritated at Boz for enjoying the womanly image of Kate, obviously naked under her bathrobe. As if Garth hadn't been doing the same thing.

"Took my mind off the pain," Boz said. "She's nice, buddy. Not nearly the bitch you and I figured her for."

"That's charitable of you, considering she coldcocked you with a jar of peanuts a few minutes ago."

"She didn't mean that peanut jar for me. I forgive her. Especially whenever she leans over me with that loose robe."

"Cut it out, Boz. She's a hotel guest."

"Aw, harmless fun, Gartho. Besides, I'm spoken for."

"Which reminds me. Want me to call Shirley?"

"Nope. Let's see how this turns out. I think she's got a kid home sick from school today. No use adding to her problems."

Garth thought of Shirley, a woman struggling to raise three children on a bookkeeper's salary. She and Boz had been dating each other exclusively for three years. Maybe problems with Shirley had affected Boz's work at the resort. "How are you two getting along these days?" he asked.

"Okay."

"You ever going to marry her?"

"Like I said, no use adding to her problems."

"But—" Garth paused as a knock sounded at the door. He got to his feet and looked through the peephole. "The cavalry has arrived," he said, and opened the door to the paramedics.

KATE HEARD the knock and quickly zipped up her slacks. The cut on her foot had stopped bleeding, but she grimaced as she pushed her stockinged feet into a pair of low-heeled shoes. Then she hurried into the sitting room. She needed to know what the paramedics had to say about Boz, whether Garth wanted her there or not. She couldn't decide what Garth thought of her. One moment she was sure he didn't like her at all, and the next she'd catch him looking at her so warmly it made her shiver with delight.

She'd been so concerned about Boz that she hadn't thought much about what she had on until Garth had made that remark about getting dressed. Then she'd realized, belatedly, that she'd probably given both of them a show while she was trying to pick up all the pieces of glass. Maybe Garth thought she'd been intentionally trying to attract his interest. She didn't want him to think that, didn't want him to guess what she'd been dreaming about when Boz, poor Boz, had come to the door.

Two paramedics were on the floor beside Boz taking his blood pressure and shining a light into his eyes. Garth stood nearby, frowning.

"I think we need to take him in for X rays," one of the men said, and the other nodded.

"I'm fine," Boz insisted. "I don't need to go anywhere."

"Better let them take you," Garth said.

"I can't leave. There's too much to do around here. Some of the help took off to go surfing today, and they're liable to take off tomorrow, too. That always happens at high tide, especially with a full moon. So I gotta look for extra bodies to fill in for tomorrow's deal."

"I'll handle it."

Boz was quiet for a moment. "Yeah, I know you will," he said. "You always do."

Kate listened with interest. When Boz had mentioned staff members who habitually left to go surfing, Garth's frown had deepened. No doubt he was angry to discover that he'd been forced into carrying her luggage this afternoon because some bellman was out riding the waves. She wondered if Garth disapproved of the way his buddy was running his resort.

"I vote with Garth that you should go to the hospital, Boz," she said, stepping forward. "An X ray would determine the extent of the injury."

"Maybe it did me some good," he said. "I could probably use a good knock on the head."

Kate walked over and knelt beside him. "Please go get it checked out," she said. "It would ease my mind considerably to know I hadn't done any permanent damage."

Boz sighed. "Okay."

The paramedics left to get the stretcher and Garth came over to crouch next to Kate. "Boz, I'm going with you to the emergency room."

"Hey, no need," Boz said, wincing as he moved his head. "This was supposed to be a little vacation for you. I know how stressed out you've been lately. It's bad enough you have to take charge here for a few hours, without adding in a trip to the hospital."

"I'm going," Garth said. His smile didn't soften the glint of determination in his gray eyes.

Kate saw the look and felt a jolt of sexual awareness. Determination was very sexy in a man, she decided. Especially in this man.

AFTER THE PARAMEDICS LEFT with Boz strapped to the gurney and Garth walking protectively by his side, Kate prowled the suite restlessly. She'd never been a prisoner before, and she didn't like it.

From her room she could see the ocean and a small strip of the beach. A woman with a bag of bread crumbs had attracted a flock of noisy gulls at the water's edge. Beyond the woman, black-suited scuba divers in groups of six or eight moved like seals through the water. She counted four such groups. A fleet of seven kayaks, each a different crayon-bright shade, launched into the surf. Laughter floated up to her as the group of kayakers paddled toward a half-moon slice of beach to the south ringed by sandstone cliffs the color of buckskin.

Kate found a hotel information brochure and learned that the kayakers' destination was La Jolla Cove, a paradise for scuba divers. The long gray pier at the other end of the beach belonged to the Scripps Institute of Oceanography. She envied the divers and the kayakers, envied even the joggers and strollers who were free to roam the beach, to dabble their bare toes in the gentle surf and hunt for seashells.

For nearly two hours she alternated between reading Garth's financial magazine, which she found boring, and observing the activity on the beach and in the water, which she found frustrating because she couldn't go outside. She felt like a little kid with the flu who had been banished to her room until she was better. In addition, she'd developed another problem. She was hungry.

She couldn't go out to eat or order room service and risk exposing her position. The peanuts were out of the question, even if she washed them and separated them from the glass. *I'd have to be starving to eat peanuts again*, she thought. An inspection of the contents of the courtesy bar turned up pork rinds, cheese-flavored crackers and marshmallow cookies. Unless she thought of some other solution, that would be her dinner. Then she noticed the small screw-top bottle of wine and decided to start with that.

Moments later, with the Chardonnay in a bathroom tumbler and the love seat positioned close to the sliding door, Kate kicked off her shoes and settled in to watch the sun disappear behind La Jolla Cove. A sweep of clouds as thin as a silk scarf blushed pink. Gradually the sky became washed with color; purple near the horizon blended upward to mauve, fuchsia and peach. The dimpled water, silver at first, took on the sheen of pink cellophane. One lone pelican skimmed the surface before flapping away toward the cliffs. A fringe of palm trees above the cove inked a jagged silhouette against the brilliant sky.

Kate's enjoyment was bittersweet. She longed to share a moment like this with someone special, to cuddle in the crook of his arm as they both gazed in silent appreciation at the sunset. What a laugh. Here she was, touted as *the* expert on sex and love, and she had neither. That was the story the press would never get. Dr. Kate was lonely.

The phone rang and she tensed. Telephones had become her enemy in the past few days. As she crossed to the end table and picked up the receiver, she decided to disguise her voice, to be on the safe side. "Allo?" she murmured in something resembling a French accent.

On the other end of the line, Garth laughed. "Interesting, Kate."

"Oh, it's you." His call, coming just when she'd been wishing for a lover, made her pulse leap, but she tried to keep her response calm. "How was my accent? If it hadn't been you calling, would you have been fooled?"

"Absolutely," he said, and laughed again. "If it hadn't been me calling, I would think I was shacked up with a French mistress."

Don't say things like that, Kate thought. *Not when I'm feeling so vulnerable to ideas like that.* "Are you calling from the hospital?"

"No, I'm back in my—your—suite."

Right above her. She glanced up and wondered if he was on the love seat, as she was, or lounging on the bed. "How's Boz?"

"He has a small concussion, but the doctor isn't too worried. She advised keeping him there overnight, for observation."

"That's probably a good idea, but where does that leave you? *Is* this supposed to be your vacation?"

There was a short hesitation on the other end. "No matter," he said. "I'll keep an eye on things for Boz until he gets back tomorrow. He'll be here in the morning, before your luncheon starts."

"Will you have to hire more people before then?"

"Looks like it. I didn't realize half the help leaves when the surf's up. Fortunately Boz has quite a few applications on file. I picked up the folder from his office before I came up here."

"You're going to be busy."

"Comparatively. Why?"

She wondered if she imagined the quickening in his voice, the note of interest. "I hate to bother you," she said, "but I haven't figured out how to feed myself."

"Oh. Yeah, I should have thought of that. Can you hold on for an hour, while I get some interview appointments set up for later?"

"Sure." Kate decided the cheese crackers and the wine would do the trick.

"Good. The restaurant makes a pretty good pasta and chicken dish. I'll bring it up in about an hour, if that's okay."

"Sounds terrific." Kate hated to admit to herself how terrific it sounded—and it wasn't just the thought of food that made her mouth water, but the thought of the person bringing the food. She decided to take a little risk. "Maybe you should bring some for yourself," she said. "I know you'll be working late tonight, but you'll have to eat sometime."

"I might just do that. Incidentally, you had a message from Stella."

"What did she say?"

"Her father's out of immediate danger but she's staying on there at least through tomorrow. She left a number. Do you want it?"

"No, I guess not. No point in bothering her. I'm sure we can handle tomorrow."

"I'm sure we can," Garth said. "Any messages for me?"

"No, everything's been quiet." The conversation had become quite cozy, Kate thought. She liked that.

"Okay, then. See you in about an hour, sooner if I can make it."

"Fine. See you then." Kate hung up the phone. *See you then, Garth.* Savoring the thought, she glanced out at the darkened balcony. The lights were off in the room, and the sky was nearly dark. She could chance a breath of fresh air, certainly. With a sense of daring, she pushed back the sliding screen and stepped out onto the balcony.

The sea air smelled like pretzels. The surf, lit by floodlights attached to the resort's roof, looked as if someone had pressed the nozzle on a giant can of whipped cream. Kate knew she was hungry when everything around her reminded her of food. Soon Garth would be bringing dinner. She absorbed the sensuous rhythm of the waves and hugged herself with anticipation. Garth would watch out for her, take care of her, guard her from harm. She wasn't afraid anymore.

BENEATH HER BALCONY and to the left, deep in the shadows, a figure waited. He'd kept his vigil for most of the afternoon, ever since someone else had answered the telephone in her room. He was rewarded by the sight of the woman.

There she was, the know-it-all bitch. Thought she could tell women all about men. Thought she could move in and spoil things for him, turn his Janey away from him. But Janey would see that this woman wasn't so great. When he told Janey how this woman had cowered before him, Janey would take him back. She'd see how powerful he was, how much he knew about women.

He knew they'd moved the bitch to a different room, but he'd expected she'd still be in one of the high-class ones with balconies. He just hadn't known which balcony. Now he did. They'd moved her a floor lower. All the better.

4

KATE RETURNED to the love seat to finish her wine, her mood improved considerably by the prospect of having company. The book tour had been a series of crowded public appearances and radio interviews followed by long stretches of time when she'd been completely alone. Even Stella, her publicist, hadn't been available for quiet chats during those down times because she had been busy confirming the arrangements for the next stop.

Kate missed her women friends, three fellow teachers at Northbluff College. The four of them had banded together as the more liberal members of a largely conservative faculty. All of them were single, although Ann lived with a guy who taught engineering and Jennie was getting pretty serious about somebody who owned a farm outside of town. Donna, the ringleader, had no current boyfriend, and consequently late-night wine-and-cheese sessions usually took place at her apartment.

Kate remembered that on the night she'd told Danforth to get lost she'd called Donna, and her friend had insisted on gathering everybody together to give Kate moral support. They'd sprawled in Donna's living room with a jug of Chablis, assorted boxes of crackers and a cheese board piled high with generous hunks of cheddar and Swiss. Kate had concentrated on the wine, trying to get drunk. She'd failed, and instead of the evening passing in a liquor-induced haze, she remembered nearly every word said that night, probably because the words had changed her life.

Donna started the Danforth-bashing session. "I always knew he was no good." She flicked an ash from her cigarette. The group also met at Donna's because she smoked and much as they all loved Donna, they didn't let her smoke in their houses. "Even his name sounds sneaky."

"Kate, I wouldn't have told you this before, but that guy was always trying to cop a feel." Ann pushed her glasses up on her nose and turned to Jennie. "Isn't that right?"

"What?" Kate cried.

Jennie's blond hair swayed as she nodded. "I counted three separate times he 'accidentally' brushed his hand against my boobs."

"No!" Kate took another gulp of wine.

"Yes! Didn't you ever notice how he'd dangle his arm over Ann's shoulder?"

Ann groaned. "I thought that went out with high school, but ol' Danforth revived the technique."

"I guess I shouldn't be surprised. Did you guys know he had that thing going with that woman in Bushnell? Don't tell me you knew about that and didn't—"

"No, we didn't know," Donna said. "We all knew he was an immature little scumball, but we didn't know that. Believe me, Kate, you're better off."

"That's for sure." Jennie raised her glass.

"To your freedom," Ann said, clinking her glass to Kate's.

"Down with rat finks," Donna added.

"Danforth be damned." Kate clicked her glass to everyone else's and drank deep. The wine didn't subdue her anger. "But why the hell didn't I see it coming?"

"We never see it coming," Jennie said. "I'm starting to wonder what I've missed about Stewart. All right, you guys. Anybody see anything wrong with Stewart?"

Donna took a long drag on her cigarette. "For a farmer, he's okay. 'Course, sometimes he smells of road apples, but—"

Jennie threw a cracker at her. "That's not what I mean. I'm talking about his character."

"Yeah, I wonder about that, too," Ann said. "I've lived with Gil for ten months, and he sounds so liberated, but sometimes he gets this look on his face, and I just know he's trying to figure out how to get me to do all the scut work around the place."

"And I'm so scared of getting a loser I just don't date anybody," Donna said.

Kate refilled her glass. "You could be on the right track. I'm sure taking a sabbatical from romance as of now." She sipped on her Chablis. "You know what we need? A user's manual for men."

"Yeah." Ann laughed. "You can find books about how to pick out a puppy, but where's one for how to pick out a man?"

"Maybe you could use the same book," Jennie said with a grin.

"I sure couldn't have done any worse if I had." Kate felt an idea nudging at her. "What if . . . what if somebody interviewed lots of women, those who are happy and those who aren't, and came up with a sort of checklist?"

"I'd read it," Donna said.

Jennie cut into the cheddar cheese. "Me, too."

"Me, three." Ann turned to Kate. "What if something like that could be used in one of your classes? Wouldn't that be great?"

"God, I wish *I'd* had a class like that, or a book like that to read."

"So write it, Kate." Donna's voice held a note of command. "Here's your chance to crack down on the Danforths of this world."

Ann nearly spilled her wine in her excitement. "Of course! Kate's the psychologist. She's the perfect one."

"I think it's inspired," Jennie said, sounding slightly drunk.

Kate looked at all of them. "I think it's insane," she said.

Yet in the days that followed she'd been unable to put the idea from her mind. At last, with repeated prodding from her friends, she'd begun the research.

Her hours of work on the book and her quiet campus life seemed aeons away from what she'd experienced in the previous two weeks, however. She should have had an inkling of what awaited her six months ago when she'd flown to New York for a make-over and photo session for the dust-jacket picture. She hadn't recognized the sophisticated woman captured on film. In preparation for the session, she'd spent an entire day at a famous New York salon, her visit paid for by her publisher.

Kate still laughed at the memory of the hairdresser and his ill-concealed horror as she'd explained that she usually tied her shoulder-length hair at the nape of her neck to keep it out of the way when she taught. The hairdresser had tossed her ponytail holder into the wastebasket, lopped off several inches of her auburn hair and given her a body perm.

She'd also received a simultaneous manicure and pedicure, although she couldn't imagine why the publisher cared about her feet. Last of all she'd been made up with a host of expensive cosmetics. When she was given the cosmetics to take back to Nebraska, she should have known that somebody expected her to use them again.

She thought of the cosmetics now and remembered she hadn't redone her makeup since she'd scrubbed it off before taking her bath. After closing the curtains over the sliding doors in both the sitting room and bedroom, she turned on the lights in the suite. In the bathroom she pushed aside the heavy makeup and dramatic eye shadows given to her by the makeup artist in favor of the subtler shades she preferred. She spritzed herself with her favorite lemon-scented cologne and returned to the sitting room as a knock sounded at the door. Garth was early.

She checked the peephole and opened the door.

"Room service." He balanced a full tray on one upraised hand and cradled an ice bucket containing a bottle of wine in his other arm.

"Here, let me help you with that," she said, reaching for the ice bucket.

He stepped back. "Nope. I'm balanced."

"You're showing off."

"Maybe." He grinned and moved around her toward the coffee table. "Or brushing up. I may have to do this tomorrow during the luncheon."

"Surely not."

He placed his burdens on the table and turned back to her. "Whatever it takes. Rusty as I am at this, I might be a hell of a lot better than some surfer I drag in off the beach."

"You didn't look so rusty to me. Nothing spilled."

"You don't know that. Maybe this is the third tray I've tried to bring up here and the first one I've had success with."

"Is it?" She liked the fact that he wasn't a braggart.

"No. I guess once you've learned how to wait tables, the skill never really leaves you." He laughed. "I guess I should be comforted by the thought that I'll never have to be unemployed. Anyway, let's eat. I got here as fast as I could because you sounded like you were starving."

"I am." The aroma of chicken coming from the steaming covered dishes made her mouth water. She glanced at the contents of the tray. "What have you got there, candles?" A romantic touch, she thought. Unless she was misreading signals, Garth had more than dinner on his mind. Well, if he wanted to lead in that direction, she certainly had no objections. . . .

"At the Pelican, we do everything with class," he said, taking a folded linen tablecloth and flipping it over a round table at the far end of the room.

"I'll be glad to help."

"You're a guest." He continued to set the table with practiced efficiency. "Just think of me as your waiter." He took a small corkscrew from his pants pocket and uncorked the wine.

"But you're not my waiter. You're the owner of the hotel. Besides, a waiter wouldn't sit down and share this meal with me."

"He would if he could get away with it."

Garth poured the wine and replaced the bottle in the ice bucket without looking at her, but she had to believe he'd paid her a compliment—which meant her assessment of his plans had to be right. "Thank you."

He produced a lighter from his pocket and flicked it over the candles. Then he repocketed the lighter and pulled out one of the chairs flanking the table. "Dinner is served," he said, glancing at her.

She smiled. "Holding my chair is unnecessary, especially in these liberated times."

"I told you to think of me as your waiter."

"But I can't," she said, walking toward the table. "Because you've already said you won't accept tips. You can't have it both ways."

"Then what would you like me to be?"

He was flirting. She knew it and he knew it. He was a tempting sight leaning against the chair, his smile beckoning, his hair already slightly tousled, his white shirt unbuttoned at the neck and the sleeves rolled back over his forearms. She wondered what he'd do if she told him that she'd toyed with the thought of him as her lover.

But she'd never been that forward with a man, despite the advice she gave in her book suggesting that women be more honest about their sexual attraction to a suitable man. However, advising other women to do it and acting on that advice were two different things. Behind the media-created image of Dr. Kate lurked a sexual coward. "Let me think about that," she said.

"All right."

"But in the meantime, let's eat." She slid into the chair he held out for her and actually enjoyed the ritual of him leaning forward to push her closer to the table. His aftershave, the scent she remembered so well from earlier in the day, wafted toward her. The old chauvinist customs might seem to weaken a woman's position, she thought, but they brought men and women into seductive proximity. Danforth hadn't been into holding chairs or doors for her, and they'd always seemed to be at arm's length from each other, as if afraid to tread on each other's territory. Garth was "in her space" as her friends said, and she found she liked it.

As Garth sat across from her she wondered if the candlelight had softened his features or if he was simply more relaxed than he'd been this afternoon. She picked up her wineglass. "Here's to a speedy recovery for Boz."

"Amen." He touched his glass to hers.

She sipped the wine and judged it several cuts above what she'd had from the courtesy bar. "You really think he'll be all right?"

"I'm no doctor, but he seems fine, and the people at the emergency room weren't acting real worried, just cautious. Boz is tough. He'll be okay."

"Good." Kate accepted the pronouncement with relief and started in on the savory chicken-and-pasta dish. After the first bite she murmured her praise. It was the first meal she remembered really tasting and enjoying since the tour began.

"Glad you like it," he said, digging into his own mound of pasta.

She took a sip of her wine and watched him eat. Such a basic drive, she thought, the need for food. Basic like sex. She took another bite of the pasta covered with a creamy herb-flavored sauce and wondered if Garth approached sex with the same gusto as he did food. If he savored the taste of a woman as much as . . . damn, she had to watch those kinds of thoughts, especially if she was too cowardly to act on them. She'd end up a frustrated woman when the evening was over. "You and Boz have been friends for a long time, right?" she asked, pushing away her erotic thoughts.

Garth nodded. "We met at a place a lot like this twenty years ago, when we were eighteen and freshmen at the University of California. We bussed tables, bell-hopped, whatever we could do to pay for tuition." He gestured with his fork toward the tray on the coffee table. "Carrying that up here sure brought back memories."

"And lugging the suitcases, too, I'll bet." It was a struggle to continue the conversation, as her attention was focused on the steady rise and fall of his chest, the flex of his forearm as he reached for the bottle of wine and topped off their glasses. She wondered what it would be like to undress him, to have him undress her.

"Speaking of those suitcases, what do you have in them—rocks?"

"Books."

"Yours?"

Kate nodded. "I know it seems silly, but I worry that I'll arrive for an autographing and there won't be any books for people."

"You didn't need to worry. There's a whole window full of them down at the La Jolla Book Bag."

In the shadows cast by the candlelight the cleft in his chin was more prominent. She imagined pressing her lips to the narrow groove. "People want the books to be right on the premises. They don't want to have to run to a bookstore and come back for an autograph."

Garth picked up his wineglass. "Good point." He took a swallow and swirled the golden liquid, gazing into it. "I can see you're service oriented. I wish Boz would be more conscious of things like that around here."

She studied his hand as it cradled the bowl of the wineglass. He held the fine crystal firmly, yet gently. She imagined that hand against her skin and enjoyed a quiver of desire. "Have you and Boz worked together all your lives?"

He set down the wineglass before he answered. "Just this past year. I—I've been a little luckier than Boz, financially. In a lot of ways, I guess. I finished my degree in economics. He ended up getting married, never graduated, had two kids."

"He's married? But—"

"Not now. He and Linda divorced about five years ago. He'd been running a health club and that went under about the time I was looking for a manager for the Pelican. I offered Boz the job."

And he's not doing it very well, Kate thought, remembering the confusion upon her arrival. But the confusion had given her a chance to meet Garth. "That was considerate of you, to help him out by giving him a job," she said.

Garth shrugged and took another bite of his pasta.

His mouth fascinated her. It was wide and generous, made for the enjoyment of food . . . and other sensual delights. She had to keep talking or she might just march over there and pull him from his chair for a full, satisfying kiss. "A resort like this must be a very expensive venture."

"Very." Garth paused. "I thought Boz would be good at running it. He likes people, likes to entertain, enjoys beautiful surroundings, good food."

Kate was astounded to realize she'd eaten most of her pasta already. "Well, he certainly must have the kitchen in hand. This meal is excellent."

"The food's about the only thing that's still first-rate around here. I'm beginning to wonder if Boz is going out surfing every afternoon, too. I mean, can you imagine why . . ." He paused and gazed at her in silence for several seconds.

"What is it?" She held her breath. Had he guessed her thoughts? Or had he been waiting until the spell of their intimate candlelight setting worked the proper magic and she was mellow enough to approach? Her heart beat faster as she imagined him rising from the table and drawing her from her chair, gazing into her eyes. Did she have the courage to accept an invitation to bed if he issued one? "I must have pasta on my chin or something," she said with a smile.

He shook his head. "You are really something, you know that?"

She felt her face flush under his scrutiny. She *would* make love to him if he asked; she'd been a prim college professor far too long. "You think so?"

"I think so. I came up here tonight with every intention of finding out more about you, and here I am about to spill my guts about my best friend. I admire your technique."

Kate's fantasies crashed to the ground. "Technique?"

"You're smooth, really smooth."

A tremor of anger went through her. She dismissed it, thinking perhaps she had misunderstood. "I don't know what you mean. I was simply making conversation."

"Sure you were." His voice was quiet but his words hit her like individual rocks. "You're a shrink, aren't you? You love getting into people's heads and poking around, finding out what all the little hidden motivations are."

"And what if I do?" She struck back, hurt and angry that he could attack her this way when she'd been having such intimate thoughts about him. "What's so wrong with being interested in people, in what's really going on with them? I do find that fascinating, and I'm not about to apologize for it! Lots of people have that same interest."

"Especially women. But most of them aren't professional brain-pickers. I'd say you have a black belt in this area, Dr. Kate, and that makes you dangerous."

She flung her napkin to the table and stood. "Dangerous to whom? What are you afraid of, Garth?"

He followed her lead and pushed away from the table. "Let's just say that for a moment I forgot you were the author of a book called *Getting the Sex You Need from Your Man*. That title says it all, as far as I'm concerned. I can just imagine how you advise women to manipulate the poor slobs they've hooked, how to pamper their egos—hell, that's probably what was just going on here! Which page is that particular lesson on, Professor?"

He didn't deserve the truth about her or her book. Not when he was willing to make such outrageous assumptions. "You must believe, quite incorrectly, that I have some interest in you as a man! Talk about an ego that doesn't need pampering!"

He stood and moved toward her, pointing a finger as he came closer. "You're right. I don't need pampering. I don't need some woman to play up to me, to play games to lure me into her bed. If I want someone, I go after her. Simple as that."

Kate had had enough of his double standard. She gestured toward the candlelit table. "Like this?"

His jaw tightened. "No, like this." Before she could react to stop him, he took her in his arms.

She hated this sort of strong-arm stuff, never believed that women could be turned on by someone grabbing them and kissing the breath out of them. Never believed it until now. Sweet heaven, but his arms felt strong and secure! The pressure of his lips fed the need that had been building in her for hours, ever since she saw this man. She wanted to reject him, to struggle out of his arms, but she couldn't make herself do it. His kiss felt too good, and she moaned with satisfaction.

This couldn't be right, she thought vaguely as her body responded to his. They'd just been arguing. He didn't respect her work, and probably didn't respect her. But respect wasn't what she craved right now. And hadn't she advised women in her book to be less puritanical?

He tasted of wine and the creamy pasta sauce that had covered their main dish. The leap from one physical gratification to another came so easily. She began kissing him back, exploring that wonderful mouth with her tongue. His scent captured her, bringing back the moments when she'd imagined him in the shower, when she'd put on his bathrobe and imagined his arms around her, just as they were now. His grip loosened and he began to caress the small of her back, her hips, her waist, the underside of her breasts. She couldn't explain her explosive reaction, didn't want to try. If only he'd keep on touching her....

And then it was over. He stepped away from her as suddenly as he'd pulled her close. He was panting, and the look in his gray eyes reflected his struggle. "That was childish," he said, struggling for breath.

She stood, dazed and confused, and worked to bring her own responses under control. "You mean the fight, or...?" She couldn't describe what had just happened between them.

"Just now." He looked at her and shook his head. "I'm no better than the other jerks you've been dealing with, the ones you said wanted Dr. Kate as another notch in their belt."

"That's what this was about?" Pain sliced through her. "You wanted to seduce Dr. Kate?"

"No! I mean, maybe, somehow, the idea that you're some sort of sexual expert has me going on some level." He ran his fingers through his hair. "I'm not proud of that but it may be true, dammit."

"I think you'd better leave." She hugged herself and fought back tears.

"Yes." He started toward the door, then turned back to her. "I'm sorry."

"So am I." *You have no idea how sorry.* She'd been so ready to take a chance, to uncharacteristically trust her instincts with this man. But he was like all the rest.

"I'll have breakfast sent up in the morning. What time?"

"Six."

He nodded and walked out the door, closing it quietly behind him.

Kate needed air. Turning out all the lights and blowing out the candles, she slid back the door to the balcony leading off the sitting room and stepped into the cool salt air. Mist rolled in from the ocean and swirled in the spotlights focused on the surf. The full moon was still hidden behind the hills, but occasionally the landing lights of a plane headed for the airport in San Diego appeared through the mist and cast a silver path along the water.

Kate leaned against the rail as the breeze cooled her flushed skin. She should have known better. She'd let physical desire interfere with her reasoning powers. Like so many other men she'd met, Garth wanted to find out what she knew and perhaps teach the expert a thing or two. He'd recently been divorced, and she knew from her counseling experience how that could affect a man. He might be antagonistic toward women in general, and especially one in particular who claimed to understand how he ticked.

Her mistake had been allowing herself to be attracted to him, which left her open to being hurt. She was almost more angry at herself than she was at him. Almost.

High waves curled in toward shore, smashed against the beach and spread across the sand like a spilled pan of soapsuds on a kitchen floor. The constant rhythm and majesty of the approaching tide mocked her petty concerns; as she gazed toward the dim horizon and thought of all that water traveling for hundreds of miles before washing onto another beach, her problems lost their magnitude.

Feeling calmed, she glanced up and down the beach, where a few late-night joggers splashed along the edge of the water. Otherwise the beach was deserted. Children had left behind a sand castle being slowly devoured by the rising tide. And just below her balcony, someone had made patterns in the sand. She looked more closely, trying to make out what they were.

Then she looked closer. They weren't patterns. Someone had written something. Once she understood the

message, Kate fled inside and locked the sliding door.
Then she closed the drapes and stood there panting as the
words played over and over in her mind. Someone had
left her a warning in the sand. The warning read See You
Soon, Bitch.

5

KATE TREMBLED in the darkness and wondered what to do. She had no doubt that the same man who had harassed her by phone had written the message in the sand, but even if he had, nothing had changed, really. She couldn't call the police just because some nut had written a message in the sand. It was close enough to the waterline that it would be erased by the time the police arrived, anyway.

Still, she wished the change in rooms hadn't moved her another floor closer to the beach. Too bad this hotel didn't have a fourth floor, or even a tenth. Too bad she couldn't be lifted by helicopter out of this place and set down—where? Maybe she simply wanted to be set back in time to the life she'd had before she'd sold her book.

Stella had warned her after the first couple of obscene calls that this sort of thing often accompanied celebrity. But Kate hadn't intended to be famous. She had only intended to exorcise the demons that had plagued her after Danforth left. She'd responded to his withdrawal as she had to any major happening in her life—she'd decided to study and analyze it.

Her interviews and observations had fallen almost naturally into book form, as her friends had predicted they would. She had hoped to use what she'd written as a textbook in a male-female relationships class; however, her publisher had had bigger plans. Kate had been flattered to learn that her discoveries would enjoy a wider audience than the students at Northbluff—she just hadn't quite figured out that the more women she reached with her book, the less privacy she'd have for herself.

She checked the door lock again and then felt her way through the darkness to the hallway door, which she was sure had locked automatically when Garth left. It was secure. Beginning to feel foolish for creeping around in the dark, she turned on the lights and began tidying the suite. She stacked the dinner dishes on a tray and put it near the door. She wasn't quite brave enough to open the door and put it into the hall. She could do that in the morning.

A copy of her book, the one she'd held ready in case she'd needed to smash Boz again, lay on the end table. She took it into the bedroom and started to put it back in the suitcase with the others. She stared down at the stacks of books in the blazing red covers; the title screamed out at her, as always. Still holding the copy in her hand, she walked over to the nightstand and left it there.

After she got ready for bed she picked it up and began scanning the pages to reassure herself that it *was* a good book, a scholarly work containing hundreds of interviews with women who'd had trouble communicating their sexual and emotional needs to the men in their lives. She'd interviewed men, too, and discovered that not all of them cared to listen to what women wanted, sexually or otherwise. Her advice, if she dared call it that, suggested women find men who would listen, and then talk—talk a blue streak.

She hadn't talked to Danforth—mistake number one—but somehow she knew he wouldn't have listened even if she'd tried. Funny, but despite Garth's prickly behavior about her profession, she had a feeling he might be a listener. At least he made no bones about his mistrust of her. Danforth had been the sneaky kind—a trained psychologist who said all the right things yet harbored a hatred of women. After all her research Kate was learning to recognize the type, and she didn't think Garth was like that. Not that it mattered. After tomorrow she'd never see him again.

Kate put the book on the bedside table, switched off the light and settled down against the soft feather pillow. *One more night*, she thought. Then she could go home for a week and rest up before doing the Jerry Perry show in L.A. Thankfully Stella hadn't been able to line up anything with the big talk show names. Her publicist had been bitterly disappointed about that; Kate had been ecstatic. She was almost finished with the publicity for her book, almost finished with being an author. Maybe soon she'd get her life back.

HIGH ON THE BEACH, out of the reach of the spotlights, a man watched as the second-floor bedroom light winked out. He crushed his empty beer can and tossed it on the sand. Then he pried another can loose from the six-pack plastic casing and flipped the top.

Eddie Gump considered himself to be tough. His mother had taught him to be. He'd learned to take her beatings without a whimper. These days she swore she'd never whipped him like that, but Eddie remembered. He didn't blame her, though. He loved his mom. She'd made him tough, and that meant a lot in a world like this, a world where some bitch could write a book and turn his Janey into one of those radical-feminist types.

Eddie had had a little trouble with school. Not that he wasn't smart, but most of the teachers were bitches trying to tell him what to do. So he'd dropped out, joined the army, learned welding. Finding a job after he got out hadn't been as easy as the recruiters had said it would be, but he got by. Whenever he got laid off, like now, he went hunting, or rock climbing. He kept in shape, which was a good thing, considering how this business with Dr. Kate was turning out.

She'd seen the note he'd left her in the sand. The way she'd acted after seeing it had been worth all the trouble he'd had writing it without anybody noticing. He'd almost had it done once when some jerko California type in a purple jogging suit had pranced by and asked what he was writing.

"Just goofin' around," he'd said, dancing all over the words so the bozo couldn't read them. The guy had laughed and told him to have fun.

Fun. Well, this was sort of fun, especially now that he knew she was scared. She'd tried to sound so friggin' sure of herself on the phone, but he'd seen how she'd scurried inside a while ago. Thought she was such a big deal, all spruced up in those outfits with the shoulder pads. Janey never used to wear those things. He'd known something was going on the first time she'd shown up in a jacket with shoulder pads. Then she'd started acting different in bed, talking about something called a "courtship phase." To hell with that. When he wanted it, he wanted it.

In less than a week Janey had turned into a real bossy broad. He couldn't figure it, until he found the book in Janey's apartment. *Getting the Sex You Need from Your Man,* by Dr. Kate Newberry. Janey wanted him to go to some big lunch thing where this bitch would be talking. He'd gone all right. Not for Janey. For himself. He had a plan.

Tonight would mark the end of his campaign. He was in luck with this high tide, because the friggin' waves made so much noise nobody would notice him doing anything. He would be glad to get out of Southern California. Too many hippie types to suit him. But first he had to get to this bitch, show her who was boss. After he'd shown her a thing or two about how a real man got it on, he'd make her write a letter to Janey, telling her to straighten up. Janey would be so damned impressed.

He finished the beer and crushed the can as he had the first. He started to reach for a third and changed his mind. He'd need to be sharp for this. Sharp and tough.

AFTER HIRING the last of the crew for the next day's luncheon, Garth returned to his room and dialed the hospital. The nurse who answered the phone on Boz's floor said that yes, Mr. Bosworth was feeling fine, that he was standing there beside her at that very moment driving her crazy. She was more than happy to put Boz on the line and asked Garth to reprimand his friend for being such a bad patient.

"Hey, buddy!" Boz's voice boomed into Garth's ear. "Come and get me. This place is totally boring."

"Hospitals aren't supposed to be a barrel of laughs," Garth said. "I take it your head feels better?"

"Like new. I always heal fast. You remember after that fight in the bar in our sophomore year how quick my nose mended? That gash on your cheek took weeks, and I was fine in a couple of days."

"God, Boz, I haven't thought about that for years. You really landed us in a hell of a mess that night."

"*I* landed us? Weren't you the guy who noticed that two football players were picking on some scrawny little dude?"

Garth laughed, remembering. "Yeah, but I never told you to take on both of them."

"I didn't take on both of them. We divided them up."

"Only after I realized you couldn't handle the situation."

"Gartho, you were right behind me. Once I said, 'Let's do it,' you were in there swinging along with me."

Garth leaned back in his chair, a smile on his face. "And then half the bar joined in. And we were all arrested. You see what memories I have of you, Boz? Togetherness in the pokey."

"Hey, buddy, the bars aren't closed yet. Come and spring me out of here and we'll hit a few on our way home."

Garth's smile faded. It was one thing to talk about the old times, quite another to stay stuck in them, the way

Boz seemed to be. "No can do, buddy. If the doc says you need to stay until morning to make sure you're okay, then I want you to do just that."

"What's the matter, you got a date or something?"

"Nope." Garth thought about the lousy way he'd handled things with Kate. "Not even close."

"Listen, now would be the time to put the moves on Dr. Kate. She's feeling bad about clobbering me, and now that we know she's not such a witch, maybe you should slip up to her room and find out if she wants to do some research for her next book. Know what I'm saying, buddy?"

"I know what you're saying, you old lech. For your information I had dinner with our Dr. Kate, and we had a little disagreement. I doubt she'd want to include me in her research."

"You picked a fight with that luscious piece of woman? What's the matter with you? You must be losing your touch."

"I didn't pick a fight." Garth squeezed his eyes shut. "Okay, maybe I did. But she was all set to psychoanalyze me."

"So let her! Hey, tell her you'll stretch out on the couch if she'll stretch out there with you. I'm telling you, if I didn't have Shirley... Well, never mind. I do have Shirley. So you blew it. How did you know she wanted to psychoanalyze you? What did she say?"

"Never mind," Garth said. He was still embarrassed that he'd been so ready to bare his soul to Kate about his problems with Boz, and he sure as hell didn't want Boz to know he'd been part of the controversy. "She's not my cup of tea, great body or not. By the way, I hired some extra guys to handle the luncheon tomorrow. Looked to me like half the staff had the day off."

"Could be. When the surf's up, I have a hard time keeping them down on the farm, if you know what I mean."

"So fire them and hire people who aren't surfers," Garth said, impatient with Boz's lack of concern.

"Not so easy. Besides, I hate this hiring and firing stuff. You know that."

"I guess I didn't."

"Yeah, you did. I told you. You said I'd get used to it."

"Oh." Garth had wanted to have this conversation with Boz, but not with his friend on the other end of a phone line. "Maybe you did tell me. Anyway, I think tomorrow's covered."

"I'll be there. I can wait tables. Hell, we can both wait tables. With me and you on the job, you probably didn't need to hire anybody. We can cover the whole joint by ourselves, right, buddy?"

"Right, Boz." Garth felt weary, but he tried to keep his tone positive. "Call when you get released in the morning. I'll have the courtesy van pick you up."

"Sure thing. Thanks for handling things while I'm not there, Gartho."

"No problem."

"I knew it wouldn't be. G'night."

Garth hung up the phone and stared at it. Had their positions been reversed, he would have been filled with questions and recommendations. Instead Boz had wanted to know how he was making out with a woman. And a hotel guest, at that.

Garth was reluctant to think about Kate again. He'd forced her out of his mind after he'd walked away from her door a couple of hours ago. He'd learned how to ignore personal problems during his prolonged divorce battle with Judith. Had he not learned it, his business would have been in a shambles for months. As it was, he kept everything up and running, and even if Judith got a big chunk, at least the remaining portion was healthy.

Compartmentalizing his life didn't come without strain, however, and he felt that strain now in trying to block out the unpleasant exchange with Kate Newberry. Dr. Kate Newberry. He had a bad feeling that he'd overreacted to her questions. Maybe she'd just been making conversation, as she'd said. But damn, before he'd known it she'd had him telling her stuff that was none of her business. That had to be because she'd manipulated him into it, didn't it?

But he could have dealt with the whole thing differently, laughed it off, salvaged the evening. And then kissing her out of anger and frustration, losing control—that had been really stupid, for a number of reasons. The key one was that now he wanted her—really wanted her. He'd have to be careful not to end up alone with her again.

She'd responded to him, too, which only made matters worse. Of course, he could expect that from a woman who'd written a book like hers. For all he knew she had guys stashed everywhere. Research partners. And yet....

What if she wasn't like that at all? What if he'd misread her? But no, he knew the breed. Judith had paraded enough of those books in front of him, quoting from them constantly. She'd psychologically bludgeoned him with those books. He'd tried reading one once, but it had been so full of feminist invective he'd hurled it across the room.

It wasn't just the books, though, that had him spooked about women; it was a whole attitude he was encountering lately. The women he'd met didn't seem to like men very much. They weren't satisfied with a simple attraction, a mutual enjoyment of each other's differences. Instead they wanted to examine the "dynamics" of a relationship, and if the dynamics were no good, they had all the damning words at the ready. Men were always the villains. And that was just the average woman, not some psychologist like Kate, who'd had years of training in the subject.

Rubbing the tension from the back of his neck, he stepped out onto the balcony of his sitting room. The waves were crashing against the beach now as the tide reached its peak. The security lights rimming the cliffs near the cove illuminated showers of sea spray as rollers thundered against the rocks.

Garth gripped the rail and felt as if he could bend the cold wrought iron with his bare hands. He hadn't had nearly enough physical exercise since he'd arrived. Maybe what he thought was sexual need was really pent-up energy that could be released with something as simple as a good tennis match. As soon as Boz felt like it, he'd challenge him. In the meantime, maybe a run along the beach would help him sleep.

In quick order he'd changed into his running shorts and a T-shirt. He took the fire stairs down, remembering as he did so the crazy trip with Kate's luggage. At the second floor he paused. He could rap on her door, see if she was still awake. He could repeat his apology. Then what? Hadn't he just told himself not to get caught alone with her again? If he rapped on her door now, they'd end up making love. Never had such a delicious prospect seemed like such a bad idea. With a snort of frustration, Garth loped down to the ground floor and out onto the beach.

He headed for the harder packed sand at the water-line, skirted the low wall that separated the Pelican's beach from the public one, and started down toward the string of lights that marked the Scripps Institute of Oceanography's pier. Along the public beach of Kellogg Park bonfires blazed in square cement fire pits placed about fifty yards apart. Garth took a deep whiff of the wood smoke. A bonfire beside the ocean at high tide, with a full moon just peeking over the hills—a terrific setting for lovers. Not that he wanted any of that ro-mantic claptrap. He thought of the candles he'd pro-vided for dinner. Okay, maybe once in a while wasn't too bad, but too much of that hand-holding, stars-in-your-eyes stuff could get a guy in big trouble.

He hadn't been somebody's lover for a long time. He'd moved out of the house he'd shared with Judith a year ago, but he and Judith had stopped being lovers long be-fore that. He'd had sexual encounters since leaving Judith, but he didn't associate any of those experiences with the word love. Women often confused sex and love; he'd found that out in the past year.

Garth's body warmed as he ran and sweat dampened his chest and back. Running—using his leg muscles—felt good, but the exercise hadn't driven the subject of Kate Newberry from his mind. He wondered if she'd confuse sex and love, or if she'd studied the subject enough to know the difference. Maybe that was the basis of his attraction to her. A knowledgeable woman like Dr. Kate would be able to enjoy a lusty session in bed without getting all wrapped up in forever-type pledges. Garth had pledged that once in his life, and it had turned sour. He was lucky there hadn't been any kids to worry about.

Beyond Kellogg Park stretched a line of multimillion-dollar homes perched above a ten-foot seawall. Garth had once fantasized about buying one and retiring out here before he was fifty. Maybe he could still do it, but he'd have to work his butt off for another twelve years to regain what he'd lost to Judith. And certainly he couldn't afford to have Boz screw up this resort for him.

Garth detoured around a few people on camp stools, fishing at the water's edge. High tide was a good time for it. He wondered if any of them came from the multi-million-dollar homes. Maybe. Being rich didn't mean forsaking simple pleasures. He and Judith had argued about that almost from the day of the wedding.

At the Scripps' pier Garth turned and headed back down the beach. He was breathing hard, and his legs felt the pleasant ache of exertion. Maybe he'd round out the run with a visit to the resort's weight room. He sprinted for a few yards and concentrated on the physical sensations of the surf pounding the beach and his shoes pounding the sand, sometimes crushing against a shell or a piece of dried seaweed. His blood coursed freely through his heated body, making him glad to be alive, glad to be a healthy, vital animal running down this moonlit beach at high tide.

But he still wanted Kate.

KATE SLEPT for a little more than two hours before she woke up again, disoriented in the pitch-black room. The closed drapes made her feel claustrophobic. Drapes weren't going to protect her from anything, she reasoned, and got up to open them. Moonlight flooded in, and she saw the sea had turned to silver. The beach was deserted, and the tide had started its retreat, but heavy waves still crashed on the shore. She could hear them even through the locked glass door.

She padded back to bed and watched the night sky for a while. A full moon always reminded her of childhood rhymes—the man in the moon, the cow jumping over the moon. She wondered if she'd ever be a mother and tell those rhymes to her children. Finding a husband had seemed simpler before she did all her research on relationships and understood how difficult the search could be. She thought again of Garth Fredericks. If only he weren't so defensive, especially on the subject of psychologists. She sighed and closed her eyes. She really needed to get some sleep or she'd be a basket case for the luncheon the next day.

She awoke to a shower of diamonds cascading over her bed, pelting her head and shoulders. Dazed, she sat up as the hard little diamonds, reflecting the moonlight, popped and crackled on the bedspread. Then she screamed. The sliding glass door had shattered when it had been twisted loose from its moorings. A man stood in the opening with a crowbar balanced in both hands.

6

STILL SCREAMING, Kate grabbed her book from the bed-side table and hurled it at the shadowed face of the man. He ducked and the book sailed over the balcony railing.

"Now, honey, don't yell and wake up the neighbors," the man said in a loud voice. "They don't want to hear our lovers' quarrel." He started to step through the opening in the glass.

She scrambled from the bed and grabbed another book from her open suitcase. She threw it as hard as she could and it caught him on the shoulder. He winced. He ducked when he saw the next book, and it smashed against what was left of the splintered glass, sending an-other spray of diamonds onto the balcony.

"Now, sweetheart, this is a nice place. Don't be breaking up all the glass just because you're mad at me."

She threw another book straight at his crotch and missed. He wanted people to think this was a lovers' quarrel! "Help, somebody!" she screamed. "Please help me!"

She heard the sitting room door leading into the hall crash open. "Kate!" Garth yelled.

The man dropped the crowbar and dived through the opening just as Garth barreled into the room.

"He's on the balcony!" Kate cried, but the man had already flung himself over the railing. She heard the thud as he hit the ground.

"Call the police." Garth turned and sprinted out of the suite, slamming the door closed behind him.

Kate picked up the phone on the bedside table and tried to concentrate on the numbered buttons. Her hand shook so much that she punched the wrong number twice and had to hang up before she finally managed 911. When a woman answered, she swallowed and gave the information with a voice that sounded nothing like her own. Then she hung up and pawed through her closet for a pair of shoes. Glass crunched underfoot as she walked around the bed and across the littered carpet.

She stepped over the crowbar and out through the opening in the sliding glass door to the balcony. A rope fashioned into a noose hung from a decorative swirl of wrought iron. So that was how he'd climbed up. She peered down at the beach below, but could see no one. The man was gone, and Garth was nowhere to be seen, either. Only her book lay below on its back, the pages flipping in the breeze.

She listened for any sounds—of someone running, or a scuffle—and heard only the swish of the waves. Lights were on in the room next to hers, and she caught a faint movement of the drapes. The people in there had heard the commotion but hadn't acted. Kate wondered if anyone besides Garth would have come to her aid. Perhaps her neighbors *had* believed they were hearing a domestic fight.

She began to tremble violently and realized she was standing in the cold night air with nothing on but a thin nightgown. Another of her books lay in a pool of glittering glass. She picked it up. The cover was torn and several of the pages creased. She could never sell it in that condition. She carried it inside and tossed it onto the bed, making the bits of glass bounce and shine in the moonlight.

A knock sounded at the hallway door and Garth called her name. She hurried to open it. "Did you find him?"

He shook his head and stepped inside, closing the door behind him. He took a step toward her. "Are you all right?"

She wanted to throw herself into the safety of his arms, but she hugged herself instead. "I'm okay."

"I picked up your book before coming back up here." He handed it to her. He was still breathing hard from his fruitless chase.

"The books were all I could think of to throw at him."

"You think very well." His tone grew bitter. "I just wish to hell I'd found the bastard."

She clutched the book to her chest as if still using it for protection. "I can't believe he didn't at least sprain an ankle when he landed."

"He's just a lucky son of a bitch. He must have hit the ground running. God, but I'd like to get my hands on him. Men like that, who prey on women, have no right to live."

His fierce words warmed her, made her feel protected.

"You have a piece of glass in your hair."

She held her breath as he gently plucked it out. For the first time she noticed what he was wearing—a thin T-shirt and skimpy jogging shorts. "You sure got down here fast."

"I hadn't gone to sleep yet." He rolled the shard of glass between his fingers. "Did you get a look at him?"

"Not a very good one." She remembered the man staring at her through the broken door. Her lips trembled and she paused to get a grip on herself. "The moonlight was behind him, so his face was in shadow."

"Can you remember anything at all?"

She tried. "His hair's sandy colored, I think, and he's about five-nine. Muscular looking." She shuddered. "Thank God, you heard me screaming."

"I heard you, all right." His expression was tight. "I'd like to know why I was the only one. The security people Boz hired must not be any damn good, either. I found one drinking coffee in the lounge. Hadn't heard a thing, but of course he wouldn't, cocooned in the lounge. We've soundproofed that baby so we can have live music and not wake up the guests. He shouldn't have been sitting in there. I sent him out to cover the grounds, although I doubt he'll find anything." He glanced down at her. "I'm sorry, Kate. This is inexcusable."

"It . . . wasn't your fault." The shock of the experience was wearing off and she felt almost naked standing there in her nightgown. "If you'll excuse me, I'll put on a robe or something. The police should be here any minute."

"Don't touch anything. They'll probably want fingerprints, if they can get any."

"Right." She hurried into the bedroom just as the wail of an approaching siren drifted in through the broken window.

GARTH CURSED his timidity and indecision. He probably should have wrapped his arms around her and comforted her. Yet he'd hesitated, unsure how she'd take a gesture like that after a crazy man had just tried to assault her. How he'd wanted to catch the jerk. Maybe he should have vaulted over the rail after him, but good sense had warned him not to risk breaking a leg and becoming totally useless. Unfortunately, taking the fire stairs had given the sleazeball enough time to make his getaway.

Kate had reacted like a true heroine, yelling like a Comanche warrior and flinging her books at the guy. But just now she'd looked like a frightened little kid, standing there in the mismatched outfit of flimsy nightgown and sensible walking shoes. He'd ached to hold her, this time not because he had sexual designs on her, but because it seemed the most human thing to do.

A loud rap on the door told him the police had arrived, and he called to Kate to warn her.

"I heard them," she called back, and appeared with the terry-cloth robe belted tightly around her and the walking shoes still on.

While one officer, young with freckles and a quiet manner, questioned them in the sitting room, another, balding and with a loud voice, investigated the bedroom. He took the crowbar, but left everything else as it was. After some negotiating, Kate was allowed to remove her clothes from the closet, the suitcase containing the rest of her books, and her cosmetics from the bathroom before the balding officer sealed off the bedroom and bath area with yellow police-barrier tape.

Finally the two officers, Kate and Garth stood near the door of the suite, Kate's belongings piled around them, while the officers completed their notes.

"I'll get you another room," Garth said to Kate, "but I don't know if I can promise you a suite. Of course, you can have your old room back, and I'll move, if you'd rather do it that way."

She looked tired. "Let's just take this stuff to your room and figure out what's best."

"Sure. Whatever you want." He'd listened with admiration to her calm answers as she'd talked with the police. He'd heard her screaming, knew how terrified she'd been, yet she hadn't let on any of that to these guys.

As the officers started putting away their notebooks, she asked how soon they expected to catch the man who'd been after her.

"We can't answer that very well," the young guy said.

Kate turned to the balding man, and Garth noticed her hands were clenched into tight fists. She wasn't as calm as she'd seemed. "But he dropped that crowbar. Now that you have something with his fingerprints on it, and some idea of what he looks like, shouldn't you be able to find out who he is?"

The officer sighed. "I wish I could tell you we should. We'll try. We'll comb the area, and we'll sure run a check on those prints, but I can't make any promises. If the guy's never been printed for anything—if he doesn't have a prior arrest—then his prints, even if we get good ones, won't match anything we have. We could be searching for a needle in a haystack."

"But you can also work with the Houston police, right?" Kate's voice was pitched just a shade higher than normal. Garth was tuned in to her enough to recognize the difference.

"Yes, since that's where the guy first showed up and started harassing you. But since you didn't get a good look at his face . . ." The officer paused and shook his head. "Houston's a big city. Lots of guys about five-nine with sandy hair and a muscular build live in Houston."

"But when he's done something like this . . ." Kate gestured toward the bedroom.

"Nobody saw his vehicle," the officer said. "Nobody saw his face. The rope's old. We'll try to trace where it came from, and we'll work with whatever evidence we have—footprints, for example—but I can't guarantee we'll come up with an ID on the guy."

Kate's shoulders slumped. "I see." She paused. "Well, tomorrow's my last personal appearance for a while. Surely he won't follow me home to Nebraska."

The younger officer glanced over his shoulder into the bedroom with its coating of shattered glass. "I wouldn't assume that, ma'am. Back home in Nebraska, you got a dog?"

Kate shook her head.

"I'd get one. One that barks a lot."

Garth saw the panic starting to build in Kate's eyes. She'd been counting on an end to this nightmare, and the police weren't reassuring her that there would be one, even in the safety of the little college town where she lived. He touched her arm. "You look beat. Let's get this stuff up to my room and figure out where you're going to sleep for what's left of the night."

She turned her head and gave him a grateful look. "Good idea."

"By the way," the young officer said, "my wife's read your book."

Kate glanced at him. "That's nice. Have you?"

He blushed, making his freckles stand out. "Some, I guess. Anyway, she liked it. So I saw you had some extras, ones you didn't throw around when that guy came in, and I was wondering if you'd autograph one. I'd buy it from you," he added quickly.

"I'll give you one," Kate said, unzipping her bag.

"Here's a pen." The officer pulled one from his pocket and handed it to her.

"Your wife's name?" Kate balanced the book against her side, the pen poised.

"Clara."

"And yours?"

The officer looked surprised. "Don, but you don't have to—"

Kate wrote quickly. Garth could see that she'd autographed the book "To Clara and Don, with wishes for a lifetime of loving companionship. All the best, Kate." She hadn't signed it "Dr. Kate Newberry," as he might have expected, or even "Dr. Kate." Just "Kate." And the message said nothing about sex. *A lifetime of loving companionship.* An emotion squeezed Garth's heart. He was very much afraid it was his least favorite emotion of all—regret.

KATE AGREED to an elevator ride to the third floor without a protest. She wasn't up to creeping up the fire stairs, even if Garth was lugging all the suitcases again. Because it was nearly two in the morning, the halls were deserted. In a way, Kate almost wished the guy would come back so she could get a better look at him. From what the police had said, she was in a double bind. Either the man had no record and would be impossible to find, or he would have a record, which meant he was an accomplished criminal who knew how to evade the authorities.

Kate realized she'd been naive in believing that lawbreakers could be swiftly caught and punished. It wasn't that easy to catch a crook, even when he'd bashed in your bedroom door with a crowbar. On the plus side of the evening, she learned that the policeman's wife had enjoyed her book. She tried to focus on the fact that the officer and his wife might have an improved chance at a good marriage, thanks to her. The young man seemed like the type who would listen to a woman's needs, and he'd even read "some" of the book—perhaps all of it. She sighed. Somehow, these good thoughts just didn't stack up against being terrorized.

She followed Garth inside the darkened suite. He set her suitcases on the floor of the sitting room and switched on a light. Kate glanced through the bedroom door. Moonlight streamed through his open drapes and fell across the rumpled sheets on the bed. It looked as if

Garth had tried to sleep and hadn't succeeded. She wondered if his wakefulness tonight had had anything to do with her. Whatever the reason, she was grateful that he *had* been awake. If he hadn't heard her scream and come to the rescue... But he had, and she was safe for the time being.

"So which do you want, this room or another one?"

She sank down on the love seat and pulled her robe closer around her. For some reason her teeth wanted to chatter, even though the room wasn't the least bit cold. "I want a shot of whiskey from the courtesy bar," she said. "On ice."

He hesitated. "I'll have to get some."

"Then never mind the ice." She knew then that she didn't want him to leave her alone. Her bravery didn't extend that far just yet. "I'll drink it straight."

"Okay. Think I'll join you." After retrieving two glasses from the bedroom, he crossed to the small refrigerator and took out one of the miniature bottles lining the door. He unscrewed the top and divided the amber liquid between the two glasses. Picking them up, he approached the love seat and handed her one. "Cheers."

She clinked her glass to his. "Thanks for saving me."

"For now. Unfortunately you're not permanently saved."

"That's the breaks." She took a swallow of the whiskey. It burned a little, but the heat felt good going down her throat. "I don't suppose I'll ever sleep soundly again in my life," she murmured.

"Maybe not." He stood by the love seat, sipping his drink. He looked a little as if he might be standing guard.

She appreciated his not brushing away her fears. She'd known men who did that. Maybe her instincts had been right, and Garth could be a listening kind of man. "I feel as if I should have . . . I don't know . . . more clothes on."

"Would you like to get dressed?"

"Not necessarily. What I need is a nice warm sweat suit. They remind me a little of those footed pj's we used to have as kids, and I always feel protected in them. Silly, huh?"

"Not silly at all. You don't have one with you?"

She shook her head. "My wardrobe's designed for flash and dash, not protective cocooning."

"Then I'll get mine." He set down his drink and went into the bedroom.

She didn't stop him. His sweat suit would be too big for her, of course, but in this case bigger might be better, more protective.

He came back with a navy bundle and handed it to her. "Try this. There are some sweat socks there, too, for your feet."

Tears sprang to her eyes. He understood. "Thanks," she said, and left to put on the outfit, closing drapes and turning on lights as she went. He hadn't made one move toward her sexually, she realized as she closed his bathroom door and began changing from her nightgown and robe to his sweat suit and socks. He seemed to sense that now wasn't the time, that a sexual advance from him, following on the heels of what she'd just been through, would be an invasion.

She tightened the pants around her waist with the string tie. When she pulled the sweatshirt over her head

she saw that it hung to her thighs. She loved the bulky
feel of it. The brushed cotton against her skin enveloped
her and made her feel secure. She didn't care that the
feeling was false, that an outfit made no difference in how
protected she was. She just wanted to cover up, as completely and thoroughly as possible. The white socks were
the finishing touch. Mittens might have helped, too, but
that would really have been ridiculous.

She returned to the sitting room and caught his slow
smile.

"Better?" he asked.

"Much. Thanks."

"Ready to think about where you want to sleep?"

The small amount of whiskey must have had some effect on her. She could state her preference without embarrassment and make certain that he understood what
she was asking for. And what she wasn't.

"I would like to stay here," she said.

"Fine. Then I'll find out which other rooms are—"

"I'd like you to stay here, too," she said, and before the
light could go on in his eyes, she added, "On the couch."

His hesitation was minimal; her relief at his easy ac-
ceptance of her plans was great. "A substitute guard
dog?" he asked with a lift of his eyebrows.

"I guess you could put it that way. To be honest, I'm
frightened of staying completely alone tonight, but I also
don't want you to think that I . . . that is, that the suggestion carries . . ."

"I know perfectly well what you're trying to say." He
leaned down and kissed her cheek in an almost broth-

erly fashion. "Now why don't you toddle on off to bed. I'll be right out here."

Her cheek felt hot where he'd touched it with his lips, and a soft stirring within her signaled that she wasn't immune to his charms, despite her recent trauma. But the stirring was soft, not insistent. She'd finished her whiskey and rose from the love seat. "You've been a pal, Garth. Good night."

"Good night, Kate."

STAYING WHERE HE WAS and watching her walk into the bedroom alone was the toughest thing he'd had to do recently. He took some comfort in the fact that she didn't close the door. He didn't, however, kid himself that she'd left it open hoping he'd walk through—either now or sometime later.

She clicked off the bathroom light, and then the sheets rustled, the same ones he'd left an hour ago to race downstairs. He pictured her sliding under the covers dressed in his baggy sweat suit and realized it shouldn't be a provocative image. But it was. He longed to run his fingers through her hair as it lay fanned out on his pillow, to slip his hand under the loose material of the sweatshirt and stroke her breasts.

Sucking in his breath, he turned away from the door as the light went out in the bedroom. He killed the sitting-room light, too, and walked over to the sliding glass door. The moon, hanging low on the horizon, paved a pathway bright as polished chrome across the dark water. Or bright as polished steel. Garth clenched his teeth against the desire pulsing in his loins.

7

GRAY LIGHT. Rain pattering. Kate rubbed her cheek against the pillow and tugged the covers over her shoulder. Burrowing. Warm and safe. Something . . . something had happened. Something she didn't want to think about. As sleep eddied around her, the image intruded—a man in a shattered doorway. Her stomach twisted with remembered fear. But superimposed over her fear was the memory of Garth—Garth coming through another door, calling out, chasing the man away. Garth asleep in the next room, on guard.

Rain pinged against the wrought iron of the balcony, a counterpoint to the gentle swish of the waves. Kate remembered that Garth had carried all her luggage back up to his suite, not knowing if he'd have to carry it all again to another room. He'd handed her a drink and remained standing, respecting the distance she'd needed.

He didn't approve of her writing the book. Had he been like many men, he would have lectured her, blamed her for getting herself into this mess. He hadn't. Instead he'd given her the warmth of his bed, the soft caress of his sweat suit against her skin. His understanding.

Gradually the soft fabric of Garth's sweat suit, which had cuddled her to sleep, began to tantalize her instead. She caught the faint scent of him whenever she moved in the bed. The material rubbed against her breasts, her thighs. She remembered the taste of his lips, the excitement of his touch, and she began to ache. The steady drip of the rain seemed to close her into this place, alone with the man who slept in the next room.

Or perhaps he didn't sleep. Perhaps he, too, was growing restless as dawn approached. Perhaps he was lying awake, listening to the liquid whisper of the rain. And thinking of her.

She moistened her lips, swallowed. A fine tremor ran through her body. "Garth?"

Her heart pounding, she waited. But not for long. He filled the doorway, his expression shadowed by the dim light. She lifted herself onto one elbow and gazed at him. Hours earlier she'd been too numb to appreciate the drape of his T-shirt over the firm wall of his chest, or the tightness of the sleeves over his biceps. She'd missed the lean strength of his legs, whorled with hair. Then he'd given her what she had most needed—compassion. Now she needed something else.

When she spoke, she knew the low note of seduction gave away her state of mind. "Were you asleep?"

"No."

"It's raining."

"Yes." He didn't move from the doorway.

He wouldn't move, she guessed, unless she made her needs specific. He would let her decide all the way. She hesitated, licked her lips again. So easy to tell other women to ask for what they wanted. So difficult to do it herself. Her heart hammered. "Garth, I . . ."

"Say it, Kate."

"I . . . want you."

He still didn't move. "In what way?"

He wouldn't make anything easy for her, she thought. "I want you to make love to me."

"And will you make love to me?"

Her hand shook as she drew back the covers and sat up. "Yes."

He came toward her then, and she saw the fire in his eyes. In the shadows his arousal had been hidden, but as he came closer she could see that the skimpy nylon of his shorts bulged, displaying his desire. Heat suffused her, and the sweat suit that had seemed so protective became and unwanted barrier. She reached for the bottom hem of the sweatshirt, pulled the garment over her head and tossed it on the floor.

He sucked in his breath. "Very effective."

"I don't—"

"Never mind." He stripped off his shirt and his shorts. "Just never mind, Kate," he said, coming to her, taking her in his arms. "This is what we both want, what we both need."

His mouth covered hers, sending her into a swirl of sensation that left her no breath for talking, no time to think of anything except his hands, his lips, the hot press of his fully aroused body.

She touched his face, stroked the prickle of his unshaved cheek, opened her mouth to the forward thrust of his tongue. He rolled her onto her back and cupped her breast in his hand. His touch was firm, knowing, relentless. Her body quickened, yearned, twisted beneath his caress. He released her mouth and took her breast, sending a spiral of desire downward to a pulsing center that swelled with longing.

Outside the rain shifted, drove against the sliding door with a steady drumming sound. Garth peeled away the sweatpants. His touch between her bare thighs was flutter soft at first, then bolder. His fingers probed and found; she arched upward, gasping for air.

He kicked the covers away and nuzzled a path down to the point where his fingers caressed her. His mouth was hot, demanding. She thrashed against the bed as he took her deeper into passion than she'd ever been. She lost all sense of where she was, who she was, and became a shooting star of sensation, throbbing in time to the pounding of the rain, a cup full to the brim, swelling . . . swelling . . . and overflowing. She cried out at the moment of release, moaned as his intimate kisses carried her through the undulating waves that followed.

Then he slid back up her sweat-soaked body and kissed her lips. He tasted of passion. "You know how to get," he whispered against her mouth. "Do you know how to give?"

Dazed, she stared up at him.

"Touch me," he murmured. "Make love to me, Kate."

The look in his eyes sent a new current of desire through her. Slowly she guided him onto his back. Moving over him, she outlined his lips with her tongue. Then she nibbled her way down his throat. She laid her hands over his heart to feel the rapid patter as she continued to swirl her tongue through the tangle of chest hair and down, past his navel to the waiting shaft. When at last her mouth closed over him, he trembled.

With each of her movements, he trembled more, until at last he groaned and reached for her. "Yes, you can give," he said, breathing hard. "Now let's finish this the old-fashioned way."

He guided her onto her back and moved away to fumble in the bedside drawer. "Boz gave me these when I got here," he said, tearing apart a cellophane wrapper.

"What if he hadn't?" Kate realized she would have made love to Garth regardless of whether they'd had protection or not. The need was that strong.

"Then I would have turned down your wonderful invitation," he murmured, moving over her. "But you see, I knew they were there." He reached between her legs and caressed her. "I was lying in the other room, remembering they were there."

"And you didn't want them to go to waste." She opened to him, wanting more than his caress, wanting to take him inside her.

"That's right." He plunged deep.

"Oh, Garth." She wrapped her arms around his waist and held on tight.

"That's the first time you've said my name since we started making love." He withdrew and pushed in again.

"That can't be true."

"It is true." He picked up the tempo. "I've been listening. Do you know who I am, Kate?"

"Yes," she said, gasping as he brought her right back to the point of no return.

"Say my name again."

"Garth." She felt herself spinning, her body tightening, ready for the explosion.

"Say it again."

"Garth." There. Yes. Again. "Garth!"

"Good." His breathing was ragged. "Good, Kate. Hold me. Hold me!" He moaned and rocked forward.

She felt the spasms of his climax ripple through her and she tightened her arms with whatever strength remained in her. Then he relaxed, and so did she. The room was completely quiet. Even the rain had stopped. Kate drifted in a haze of pleasure. Somewhere deep in her subconscious she registered that from this moment on, her life would never be the same.

THE BEDSIDE PHONE RANG, startling them out of a half sleep. Still holding Kate, Garth reached over and picked up the receiver. "Fredericks."

"Mr. Fredericks? This is Tina down at the desk. Sorry if I woke you."

"It's okay." Garth glanced back at Kate. She was watching him with a small smile on her face. His body tingled as he remembered the sensation of making love to her. Once he got off the phone, he'd probably do it again. "What's the problem, Tina?"

"Some reporters are here. They want to talk to Dr. Kate."

"Oh." He covered the mouthpiece and turned to Kate. "Did you have any interviews scheduled at—" he squinted at the bedside digital clock "—seven-fifteen in the morning?"

Kate shook her head. "First one's at eleven-thirty," she whispered.

Garth took his hand from the mouthpiece. "Tina? I've checked the schedule and Dr. Newberry isn't supposed to do any interviews until much later this morning."

"Okay. Just a minute, Mr. Fredericks." Tina clicked off.

Garth glanced at Kate. "Ever had the press show up for breakfast like this?"

"No. Garth, don't let anyone know that I'm here with you."

He grimaced. "Don't worry. I have no desire to spend the day with microphones being shoved in my face, asking me if the rumors are true about me and Dr. Kate. You may like that sort of thing, but I— Hello? Tina?"

"The reporters say that someone broke into Dr. Kate's room last night. Is that right? I just came on duty so I haven't—"

"We had a small problem last night," Garth said, cutting her off. "The police are handling it. Nothing major. I can't imagine why the press would be interested." Next to him Kate stiffened.

"I'll see what they say about that, Mr. Fredericks," Tina said.

Damn. Garth glanced at Kate and imagined her facing a voracious mob of reporters, having to relive her nightmare.

"They're here about the break-in, aren't they?" Kate looked pale.

"Yeah." Belatedly he considered how this would affect the Pelican's reputation. People might get the idea that the hotel was unsafe. Why hadn't Boz hired a top-notch security company, instead of some cut-rate out-fit?

"They work fast," Kate said.

"Yep." He turned back to the phone as Tina came back on the line. "What'd they say?"

"They're prepared to wait as long as they have to. They want an interview with Dr. Newberry. They've also asked to talk to Mr. Bosworth, but I knew he wasn't in—that's why I called you."

He grimaced. Just what he needed, to be talking to reporters when he should be supervising the luncheon preparations. But none of this was Tina's fault. "You did the right thing," he said. "Listen, I'll be down as soon as I can get there, but I'll make no guarantees as to whether Dr. Newberry will give them an interview."

"Shall I ring her room? I wasn't sure where she—"

"That's okay, Tina. I'll notify Dr. Newberry before I come down. Offer the reporters some coffee and save a cup for me." He hung up the phone, flopped back on the pillow and stared at the ceiling. "Welcome to reality."

She touched his chest, her hand soft, reminding him of how sweetly she'd made love. "I'm sorry about all this."

He turned his head. "All?"

"Well, no." A smile caught just the corners of her mouth.

He couldn't believe she was the same woman who had stepped out of the limo yesterday looking brittle and plastic. Was it only yesterday? God, it seemed years ago. But this woman beside him was tousled and warm, washed clean of makeup and smelling deliciously of sex.

She touched his mouth with the tip of her finger and he realized he must have been smiling back at her.

"What are you thinking?" she asked, stroking his bottom lip until it tingled with the need to kiss her.

"That you are two different people. I like this one better."

She took her hand away and a chilly silence settled between them. "You're making assumptions again. Unfounded assumptions about me."

"Look, Kate, you wrote the book, didn't you?"

"Yes, I wrote the book."

"Then you must have imagined some of this merry-go-round. Maybe not having some sleaze after you, but the publicity, the image making, the loss of privacy. That's part of the game."

"You may not believe me, but no, I didn't visualize this when I wrote the book."

He made an impatient noise in his throat. "Come on. You're not that naive. Not if you're the author of a book called *Getting the Sex*—"

"I didn't choose that title, dammit!" She scrambled away from him and out of bed. "I didn't even have the chance to approve it." Naked, she marched into the sitting room and returned bearing a small case and a larger suitcase.

"Going somewhere?"

"Don't I wish. I wish a lot of things, such as I wish I'd read the promotion clause in my contract more carefully."

He tried to focus on what she was saying, but publishing information just didn't interest him when he was being confronted with his first good view of her unclothed body—slender legs, rounded, womanly hips, nipped-in waist and full breasts heaving now with indignation. He grew hard—futilely hard considering her anger and his promise to hurry downstairs and face the reporters. He tried to imagine what she was doing with those suitcases.

"But I'm stuck with the situation, and you're judging the book on the basis of that lousy title," she continued, setting the largest one down. "And you're judging me, as well. When something like what happened last night contradicts your prejudgment of me, you can only conclude that I have a split personality. Well, up yours, Fredericks!" She picked up the suitcase again, whirled and stomped into the bathroom. Once there, she plopped both suitcases on the tiled bathroom floor, and slammed the door behind her.

He stared at the closed door a moment. "But you're the author!" he called after her. "How can they change the title of your book without asking you?"

She yanked the door open and stuck her head out. "You know precious little about publishing." She slammed the door closed again. "Or women," she added, popping her head out one more time before she banged the door closed and snapped the lock.

"Hey, just a minute!" He climbed out of bed and stood in front of the door. "You can't hog the bathroom. I'm supposed to be downstairs in a few minutes."

"So am I." Water drummed against the shower stall.

"You don't have to go. I told them—"

"I heard what you told them," she called, her voice muffled by the spray of water. "But I have to face the music sooner or later. Might as well be sooner."

"But—"

"The word is, you don't have to fight my battles for me anymore," she said, cutting him off again. "Not mine, or the other woman's, that person you think I turn into when the moon is full or something."

Garth stood by the closed door and scratched his head. "I must have said the wrong thing," he mumbled.

GARTH PULLED ON his T-shirt and shorts and spent the next half hour sprawled on the love seat in the sitting room. Okay, so he didn't understand publishing, but Kate must have agreed to that title at some point. How could she have missed the ramifications? Or maybe she'd thought being famous would be fun, and too late had discovered the down side. As to her charge that he didn't understand women, he'd go along with that. When he'd mentioned he liked one side of her personality better, he'd been trying to pay her a compliment. He wanted her to know that he could put up with some of the "Dr. Kate" stuff *because* of this softer side. He was trying to look for compromise, while she apparently wanted to fight.

By the time Kate emerged, preceded by a whiff of lemon cologne, he looked up and felt justified in having made the comment she'd found so offensive. He'd been right all along. She *was* two people, and this was the one he'd seen get out of the limo.

She wore a dress and coordinating jacket, both looking as if they might have come from one of the trendy shops in La Jolla. The dress was pink with little white dots all over it, and the jacket was white. Her shoes were pink to match the dress. Not many redheads he'd seen could wear pink that well, but she had the right auburn shade that made the combination dynamite. And dangerous.

Her formerly tousled hair had been shampooed—he could smell the coconut scent—and artfully styled. It was swept back from one ear to reveal a large pink earring the size of a silver dollar anchored to her earlobe. Mascara, eyeliner and shadow made her brown eyes look deeper. Someone in the right frame of mind might think they looked mysterious and sexy. He preferred suspicious. Her mouth was made up to kiss-me-not perfection in a shade of pink to match the dress. Three pink bangle bracelets on one wrist clicked as she moved the briefcase she carried from one hand to the other and checked her watch. "The bathroom is yours," she said.

"Thank you," he said with elaborate care. "Looks like Dr. Kate is ready." It was a low blow, but he didn't care at the moment. She'd taken an innocent remark on his part and turned it into something that carried deep significance, the way he'd expected someone with her training to do. Maybe she'd even planned the fight with him. She'd gotten the sex she wanted, and maybe she also wanted to leave the resort this afternoon without any loose ends. Garth decided he'd been used.

Her mouth tightened. "I'd appreciate it if you'd have the books that are salvageable sent down to the room where I'll be autographing, in case for some reason we need extras."

"Certainly." He bowed his head, a gesture befitting the minion of a celebrity.

Her grip tightened on her briefcase. She cleared her throat. Obviously she had something else to say, but was reluctant. He had an idea what it might be, and he took satisfaction in watching her squirm.

"I, um, can't stop you from saying anything you want to the press," she said, finally, "but I would appreciate it if this . . . interlude . . . between us didn't become public."

"I would think that would be exactly what you'd want. You've just demonstrated how it's done."

Her eyes narrowed. "I beg your pardon?"

"I'm talking about credibility. How do you expect your readers to believe you unless you show them that you can get the job done? I can testify that you are very good at getting the sex you need from—" He ducked as she swung the briefcase at his head. Then he leapt to his feet and grabbed her wrists. "But I won't be giving you any added publicity, I'm afraid."

She trembled with anger. Under her makeup her cheeks were bright pink. "You think I *wanted* you to?"

"Actually, no." His grip was tight. Even now, despite all his misgivings, he longed to take her in his arms and kiss her until their hearts were pounding and their bodies sweating, the way they'd been only a short while ago. He had to admit that sex appeal oozed out of her. Maybe she had secrets to reveal to other women, after all. "I don't really think you want me to kiss and tell. I imagine you want to reserve that right for yourself, when the timing is right, say when *People* magazine comes for an interview."

Her voice was choked with outrage. "Let me go."

"But I'm warning you that if I read about us somewhere, or hear the story has titillated the audience of some talk show, I will make you very sorry. I never want my private life to be invaded. Do you understand? Never."

"You are such a jerk."

"Apparently. And as long as you think I am—" He couldn't help himself. The temptation to mess up that perfectly drawn mouth, as well as take the edge off this ridiculous hunger, was too much. Before she could guess what he had in mind, he grabbed her upper arms and hauled her in. She tasted smooth and creamy, like cherry pie. She pushed against his chest, but with less and less force as he thrust his tongue between her teeth. He was taking a chance, she could bite him. But she didn't. Apparently he affected her as much as she did him. He steeped himself in the satisfaction of that for a few more seconds before he let her go.

"I hate you," she said, backing away from him. She was breathing hard, and her lipstick was smeared. Her eyes were bright and for a minute he wondered if there were tears in them. Probably not. She was too sophisticated for tears at a time like this. "I hate you more than any human being in the world."

"Why, because I'm telling you the truth about yourself?"

She put her briefcase on an end table and fumbled through it for a small bag. She unzipped it, took out a tissue, mirror and lipstick, and repaired the damage. She put the stuff away and straightened her shoulders. Her face was a blank. She was Dr. Kate once more. "You wouldn't know the truth if it grabbed you by your private parts," she said.

He almost laughed. That was good. "I think it did," he said.

She took a step toward him, her hand upraised. Then slowly she lowered her hand and turned toward the door without another word. She left, closing the door quietly behind her.

He admitted to being a little disappointed. He much preferred the passionately angry version of Kate to the controlled one who had walked out the door. Well, that was that. End of story. He'd see to it that the luncheon went off according to schedule and then Dr. Kate would be winging her way back to wherever she lived. Nebraska. Then he could concentrate on Boz and the problems at the Pelican. He could hardly wait to get her out of his hair.

But as he walked back through the bedroom past the bed with its sheets tossed as if by a tropical storm, he knew that he was kidding himself. He'd had a small sampling of what this woman had to offer and it had only whetted his appetite. Destructive as he believed the urge to be, he wanted more.

8

I SHOULD NEVER have gone to bed with him, Kate thought as she hurried down the carpeted hall toward the elevator. All her training in psychology should have warned her against such an impulsive move. Worse yet, in her book she'd advised caution in choosing a sexual partner. She'd emphasized that getting the sex one needed— and she had used that phrase only once—started with finding the right man to give it.

She'd deluded herself about Garth, willingly deluded herself with his seeming empathy toward her feelings about the break-in. Then she'd allowed the coziness of waking up to gentle rain outside, the memory of kissing him and her own neediness to override her good sense. Maybe she'd been a victim of post-traumatic stress disorder. But when he'd made that remark about her being two people, and preferring the one he had in bed . . . the sheer arrogance of it made her tremble with renewed fury.

She jabbed the Down button on the elevator. The most humiliating part of this sordid mess was that she still wanted him. If he'd kept his damn mouth shut and hadn't made such a stupid remark, she'd be plotting ways to be alone with him again before she left for Nebraska. But he *had* opened his mouth, and driven by passion though she might be, she couldn't have a relationship with a man who stubbornly insisted that her book was a treatise on how to manipulate men—when he hadn't even read a word of it!

The elevator bell dinged and the doors slid back to reveal a car full of women. Each pair of eyes widened, and practically in unison they chorused, "Dr. Kate!"

Kate took a deep breath and pasted a smile on her face. "Hello," she said. Another day of standing in the spotlight had begun, this time a little earlier than normal.

The women in the elevator proved to be like all the others she'd met on the tour. They'd read her book and felt as if she could be their best friend. During the writing of the book, Kate had actively searched out such women, had been happy to hear their stories, but now she'd grown a little weary of being a public listening post. In the fifteen-second elevator ride she heard about two rotten husbands and one inconsiderate boyfriend. None of the men, the women reported with indignation, had been willing to read Dr. Kate's book. *It's a common problem*, she thought as the elevator bumped to a stop on the main floor.

The elevator doors opened onto a polished floor of brick-colored tile. Directly across from Kate was a gleaming cherrywood registration desk, and to her left high arched windows looked out on the ocean. A sofa grouping in a heavy mission style softened with plush cushions faced the windows. There, reporters from two television stations and one newspaper had gathered; having rested their Minicams on the floor, they sat on the sofas looking bored, flicking cigarette ashes in the palm trees and rubber plants placed amid the grouping.

A wide hallway to their left led to the dining room and banquet facilities, according to a sign jutting out from the wall. The reporters had positioned themselves so that she couldn't have coffee until she'd run the gauntlet of their microphones and camera lenses. A chrome pedestal sign standing near the hallway announced in white plastic letters on a black background that Lunch With Dr. Kate would be at twelve-thirty in the Spindrift Room. Kate took a deep breath and headed for the crowd of reporters.

Several looked up as she approached, and their expressions quickly changed from boredom to avidity. The group suddenly surged forward, adjusting Minicams and mikes as they came. Kate felt like a deer caught in a clearing during hunting season. The lights mounted on the Minicams made her squint. Microphones that looked like snake heads reared in front of her. She began to perspire. Suddenly she didn't know how to stand, where to put her hands, or whether to smile or remain serious. This happened to her every time—it hadn't become noticeably easier after ten days of the same routine.

This time was a little different. Instead of asking her about her book, they asked about the break-in. Did she think books like hers promoted violent reactions in men? How had she deterred her attacker? Did she think he'd planned to rape her? Had she sought rape counseling? Did she wonder if simply carrying the book around would endanger women who'd purchased it? Knowing that she'd attracted this kind of unwanted attention, was she sorry she'd published the book? *Yes,* she wanted to shout at them as her head began to pound. *If I'd known any of this would happen, I wouldn't have written a word!*

Then she looked into the faces of the women who had ridden the elevator with her, who had been on their way to breakfast and had stayed to listen. Others had emptied out of the elevator and joined them, drawn by the excitement of the television cameras. Kate couldn't say that she regretted writing the book, not when these women believed in her, found strength in her. They must not learn what a coward she was. It might rob them of all hope.

"I will not be terrorized out of saying what I believe about men's and women's relationships," she said. "This man's reactions prove that this book is needed, and I'm pleased that it has found such a wide audience."

From the women's muttered comments, Kate decided this was the first they'd heard that some man had been threatening her for several days. Stella had kept a lid on the information. Kate longed for Stella now. She'd know how to handle the media, how to extricate Kate after a reasonable number of questions. Had Stella been around the night before, nothing would have happened with Garth. Kate added Stella's absence to her growing list of justifications for what seemed like a really stupid move on her part.

As the questions continued, Garth stepped off the elevator. Kate didn't know until that moment that she'd been watching the elevator doors and waiting for his appearance. He carried her suitcase full of books, which he handed to a bellman, and pointed in the direction of the room where she'd be autographing later. Then he straightened his shoulders and buttoned his charcoal sports coat.

As she watched the authority and confidence with which he walked toward the crowd gathered in the lobby, Kate's stomach clenched and she had to ask a reporter to repeat a question. Only hours before, in the faint, forgiving light of dawn, she'd touched and been touched by this man in intimate ways that made her quiver with the memory of it. Kate's heart hammered as he drew closer. She had to make her escape or risk having some shrewd reporter pick up the vibrations between her and Garth.

With a feeling that she was turning him over to a pack of hounds, she gestured in his direction. "Here's the owner of the hotel, Garth Fredericks. Perhaps he can shed more light on the incident."

Lugging their equipment like recalcitrant babies, the reporters and cameramen abandoned her and headed in Garth's direction. She met his wry glance with her chin lifted. She'd taken the first wave; he could handle the second. With an acknowledging nod at her, he turned and smiled into the cameras.

The women who had gathered didn't swarm over to Garth when the reporters did. They remained to voice their outrage against the man who had been threatening Kate. Although Kate tried to deflect the questions, the women demanded to discuss the incident and to express their anger.

"I'd like to see him show his face in here today," a stout gray-haired woman announced. "We'd rip him to shreds, wouldn't we, ladies?" Heads nodded and further threats were mumbled.

Kate smiled in spite of her tension. Garth might have been some protection the night before, but this group was as good as an army. Nothing would happen to her as long as they were around, although she felt a little over-whelmed at the blend of perfumes assaulting her and the sheer psychological weight of the women's admiration.

"What is wrong with these guys?" asked a thin woman with a persistent smoker's cough. "My husband would never threaten Dr. Kate, but he's mad as a hornet about this book, and he hasn't even read it yet."

"Well, sometimes it's the way we present our needs to men," Kate began. *And sometimes it's the title of the damned book,* she thought, although she'd never said so publicly. Garth had been the only one besides her agent who knew that she wasn't in love with the title.

"Men!" said another woman, this one about thirty and dressed in a blazer and slacks. "They should all be strung up by their—"

"Julie!" remonstrated one of her companions.

"Well, they should. I haven't found any good ones yet. All of them have an overload of testosterone. If they aren't personally committing violence against women, they swear we're exaggerating. But we're not. Look at the slasher movies. Look at the headlines. Look at what happened to Dr. Kate. They're all trying to dominate us, keep us subservient through fear and intimidation."

Kate winced. "That's a pretty wide generalization," she said. She thought of Garth's solicitous behavior af-ter her terrible experience, of his anger against her attacker. He didn't approve of her book, but he'd hated the idea that some man would assault her because of it. "I've known men who are very upset about the rise in violence against women."

"Oh, they may say they're upset, but they still want to keep us in our place, and if we're scared, we'll stay in our place," the woman named Julie said. "I think they give tacit approval in subtle ways."

"Some men may be like that, but not all of them," Kate said. "As I mentioned in the book, you have to search for the ones who aren't."

"I haven't read your book yet," the woman named Julie said. "From the title, I figured that you tell us how to manage these jerks. You know, since we can't live without them, you tell us how to live with them."

"Not exactly," Kate said. "Now if you'll excuse me, I need a cup of coffee." She listened to the flood of offers to buy her breakfast. There would be no escape this day.

The exuberance of her fans was one reason why she normally had breakfast in her room and didn't appear until the autographing began at eleven-thirty. She could have done that again and allowed Garth to handle the flak, but then she would have been indebted to him. She didn't want that, not now. "Let's go see what the restaurant has to offer," she suggested, and led the swarm of women through the lobby.

They skirted the pack of reporters who still surrounded Garth and plied him with questions. Kate could imagine what he thought, dealing with those questions as she walked by trailing her retinue.

A reporter, possibly inspired by the sight of Kate and her string of admirers, asked in a loud voice, "Have you read Dr. Kate's book, Mr. Fredericks?"

"No."

"Do you plan to read it?"

Kate paused, probably masochistically, she thought, to hear what he said.

"No, I don't. It's my personal belief that such books create more problems than they solve."

Kate's shoulders slumped.

"Mr. Fredericks, are you saying that you blame this book for—"

Kate clenched her jaw and hurried toward the restaurant, not willing to whip herself any more. Garth was apparently ready to lay the responsibility for the break-in directly on her shoulders, and in another moment the reporters might turn and ask her if she agreed with his assessment. If that happened, she might say something totally unprintable.

"No, you misunderstand. I'm not blaming the book for what happened here," Garth said, watching Kate sail by surrounded by her loyal followers. They looked as if they would have liked to hoist her on their shoulders and carry her to the restaurant. It must be an author's dream, he thought, to be idolized so by readers. Kate certainly glowed under the attention. She looked regal and thoroughly in command, as befitted someone elevated to the level of guru.

Another question forced his attention back to the ring of lights and microphones surrounding him. "Would you repeat that please?" he asked.

"Why not blame the book, since it seems to have caused this reaction from the man who tried to attack Dr. Kate?"

"Because I believe in the First Amendment," Garth said. "Dr. Newberry has the right to publish her book. I may not like it, but neither I nor anyone else has the right to persecute her for it. When I said a book like that creates problems, I meant problems with relationships. I wasn't referring to criminal behavior. Guys like the one we dealt with last night aren't to be tolerated in our society."

"Have you had other break-ins at the Pelican prior to this?"

"Not under my ownership." No one in this group was cutting him any slack. "I can't speak for the years before that."

"Would you say your security measures are adequate?" another asked.

"Yes." Garth kept a tight rein on his temper. "Our security is fine," he added, stretching the truth to save Boz's reputation. "Having Dr. Newberry here created an added risk that we thought we had covered, but obviously the individual was more determined than we made provisions for. As any police officer will tell you, it's difficult to anticipate what criminals will do, because they operate outside of our normal understanding."

"But—"

Garth cut him off. "Let me assure you that the Pelican is a very safe hotel, a family hotel. We can't let the actions of one deranged individual destroy the decent atmosphere of the Pelican. We pride ourselves here on clean, wholesome fun for the entire family. The Pelican promotes a certain air of dignity that—"

A motion to his left, near the entrance, of hands waving to get his attention, made him turn. There stood Boz, his head shaved and bandaged, wearing the beach bum outfit he'd had on when Kate had clunked him with the peanut jar. So much for dignity. If the press found out about what Kate did to Boz by mistake, it would be *National Enquirer* time. "Well, I think that about wraps it up," Garth said, turning away from Boz and hoping the reporters and cameramen would do the same.

They didn't. Boz had attracted their attention, too.

"I thought you said Mr. Bosworth wasn't available?" one reporter said to Garth. "Isn't that him over by the front entrance?"

Garth wanted to deny knowing the strange fellow with the bandage, but it wouldn't have done any good. The bevy of media people were already moving in Boz's direction, and Garth had to push a couple of people aside to get there first. "This man had a minor accident yesterday and is in no shape to be questioned."

"Oh, hell, Garth, I'm fine," Boz said, slapping Garth between his shoulder blades. "A little jar of peanuts isn't enough to keep me down."

Garth winced. He could almost see the media people begin to salivate. "Boz, I think maybe it would be better if—"

A woman reporter elbowed Garth aside and stuck a microphone in Boz's face. "Could you explain that remark about the peanut jar, Mr. Bosworth? And what happened to your head?"

"Boz . . ." Garth cast him a weary glance.

"What can it hurt?" Boz said. "Makes a great story." The cameras rolled as Boz the storyteller launched into his routine. Garth tried not to think of what this would do to the Pelican's reputation as a family hotel. Or what it would do to Kate. She was really in for it now.

A few minutes later the television crews left looking very happy.

Garth faced his friend. Good old Boz had had a terrific time with the press. His cheeks were ruddy with excitement. Garth thought of the time Boz had won the chug-a-lug contest in college and had been the hero for the weekend. "I thought you were going to call for a courtesy van?" Garth said.

"Nah. Just took a cab." Boz's blue eyes looked a little bloodshot, but he flashed a pleasant grin at Garth. "That interview was fun. By the way, what were the TV people doing here so early?"

"And well you might ask. I wish you *had* asked before you told them how Dr. Kate coldcocked you with a peanut jar. The guy that's been threatening her paid a visit last night, broke into her room."

Boz's eyes widened. "No joke? Was she—is she okay?"

"Yeah. Luckily I heard her yelling. She threw copies of her books at him and managed to hold him off until I got there."

"You caught him?"

"No, but I think I scared the hell out of him. I doubt if he'll be back."

"Boy, that's good." Boz shook his head. "A lot's been going on around here."

"Yeah, and all of it will be on the six o'clock news." Garth couldn't hold his irritation back any longer. "What the hell did you have to tell them that peanut jar thing for? Couldn't you have said you slipped in the bathtub? For God's sake, Boz, you're the manager of this place. How's it going to look, you standing here telling a story about getting clobbered on the head by the country's leading sex expert?"

A wounded look came into Boz's eyes. He shifted his weight and looked away from Garth. "Guess I goofed again, old buddy. Sorry about that, but it's such a good story. I had the nurses rolling in the aisles when I told it. Sold some more tickets to the luncheon, too. Some of the gals want to come and see the woman who laid me out like that. They said maybe that's her secret to getting the sex she wants from a man. She beans 'em first, so they're semiconscious and don't know quite what they're doing."

Garth wished he were semiconscious. In fact, he must have been this morning to have considered climbing into bed with Kate Newberry. He'd probably lit into Boz partly because he was so mad at himself. The Pelican was in enough of a precarious position right now without having another skeleton hanging in the closet. With the way the press was pumped up about Kate, all it would take was the slightest hint that something had gone on between her and the owner of the hotel, and *that* would be on the six o'clock news, as well.

He laid his hand on Boz's arm. "Listen, I'm sorry for chewing you out like that." He glanced over Boz's shoulder and made sure the last of the reporters was out the door. "I guess I'm on edge. I did something pretty stupid last night, myself." He exchanged a glance with Boz. They'd been friends a long time, and a glance was all it took for Boz to know exactly what he meant.

"Well, I'll be damned," Boz said softly. "So things are pretty chummy, then?"

"No." Garth jammed his hands into the pockets of his slacks. "As you might guess, afterward she took exception to something I said. Hell, I don't know, maybe she planned it that way. Maybe she got what she wanted and then picked a fight so she could make a clean break. After all, she wrote the book on the subject."

Boz shook his head. "I don't think she's like that. What did you say to her?"

Garth didn't want to talk about it anymore. Thinking about this morning made his head hurt. "It doesn't matter. I'll just be glad when she's gone. A public figure like that is a walking time bomb around here."

"Maybe," Boz said, studying Garth. "But I—"

He was interrupted when Jeff Manges, who was in charge of banquets for the Pelican, hurried out of his office and approached them. "Three more waiters just called in sick."

Garth looked at him. "How's the surfing today, Jeff?"

"Understand it's pretty good, Mr. Fredericks. Not right here, of course, but down in San Diego I've heard that—"

"Do you believe those three waiters are really sick?"

Jeff looked uncomfortable. "I couldn't say."

"When they come back I want doctors' notes from all of them. Then I want you to check things out with the doctors. If anything sounds fishy I want you to fire them. Understand?"

Boz cleared his throat. "Listen, Gartho, I wouldn't take that kind of action if I were you. First thing you know we won't have any waiters or busboys, and then—"

"I think we're better off with nobody than people who'll desert us in the middle of an important event to go surfing."

"Aw, come on, Garth. Don't you remember what it was like to be twenty years old, riding the waves? You're only young once."

Garth eyed his friend. "Considering the way we've both been behaving recently, I'm beginning to wonder."

"Hey, ease up on yourself, old buddy. I have to admit that she's—"

"Never mind." He clapped Boz on the shoulder. "We're a few waiters shy. That means you and I are going to work this luncheon." He glanced at Jeff, who was standing there with his mouth open. "Fit us both out in tuxes. Give us a quick rundown on the setup and the menu.

And put out the word that we're still hiring. Maybe I can find someone who thinks more in terms of hanging in than hanging ten."

Jeff's mouth closed and his body snapped almost to attention. "Yes, sir, Mr. Fredericks."

9

DR. KATE, or as the reporters now called her, "Calamity Kate," sat behind a linen-covered table in a windowless room called the Sandpiper. It was almost twelve-thirty and the room was still full of women wanting copies of her book signed and reporters trying to interview her during the autographing. That was how she'd found out that somebody had leaked the story about Boz and the peanut jar.

She'd lost track of how many different reporters had introduced themselves. Some had been sent from newspapers and TV stations in the L.A. area—one had even come from Yuma, Arizona. She couldn't remember ever being so bone tired. She hadn't been alone once since she'd stepped off the elevator this morning, unless she counted the time she'd rushed into the women's rest room and hidden in a stall for five minutes.

Her fingers ached from signing autographs; her cheeks ached from smiling, and she hadn't even given her speech yet. But she couldn't disappoint the women who were standing patiently in line to meet her, who had driven here from all over the state and neighboring states to hear her speak.

She wondered who had told the press about the peanut jar and could only think of one culprit, one person she'd left facing the cameras and the microphones, one person who might have decided to do her in—Garth. Maybe this was how he was paying her back, and if he'd told them that, what else might he have said? Her heart pounded as she fielded the questions. Only the story about her knocking Boz unconscious seemed to have surfaced, but that was bad enough.

Her speech was scheduled to take place before the luncheon. A few minutes after twelve-thirty the banquet manager, who introduced himself as Jeff, came in to get her and clear the room. He promised the women that Dr. Kate would be back to sign autographs after lunch. She wondered if he realized she had a three-thirty plane to catch.

She made another quick trip to the bathroom, which was blissfully empty at last. Of course it was empty, she thought, because they were all in the banquet room waiting. Waiting for her. She felt the pressure of their expectations pushing on her shoulders, causing an ache in her neck. This was the last time. Soon she'd be on a plane winging her way back to anonymity. Even as she thought that, she doubted it was true, but she wanted it to be true so much she could taste the freedom.

She reapplied her lipstick and blush, touched up her eye shadow and powdered her nose. The large pink earrings hurt her earlobes, but Stella had insisted that they belonged with the outfit and besides, Dr. Kate couldn't wear dinky earrings. Kate closed her briefcase and put a hand over her nervous stomach. One last time.

Outside the banquet room she paused and listened to the hum of humanity drifting through the closed double doors. The hallway smelled of broiled chicken. Of the ten lunches she'd eaten, or mostly not eaten, eight of them had been broiled chicken.

From the corner of her eye she saw someone coming down the hall from the kitchen hoisting a tray full of water goblets one-handed over his head. She turned and stared at Garth dressed in a pleated shirt, black bow tie, cummerbund and black tuxedo slacks. The action of carrying the tray made him look even more broad shouldered than he was. As he'd said he might, he was waiting tables today.

She squashed the warm feeling that seemed to spring up in her unbidden whenever she caught sight of him. She remembered that he had sabotaged her with the reporters. "Did you have to tell them about the peanut jar?" she said when he was close enough that she didn't have to shout the question and risk attracting attention.

He stopped and shifted his weight, balancing the tray like an expert. "For what it's worth, I tried to—"

"You must not have tried very hard." Her attraction to him made her angry at herself, angrier still at him. "I guess you couldn't resist, could you? I'll bet you'll laugh your head off to know they have a new nickname for me. Now they're calling me Calamity Kate!"

His expression closed down. "Good name," he said, and walked past her to push open the door. "Allow me, Dr. Newberry."

How she longed to push him, upsetting his delicate balancing act just enough to send him sprawling, tray of drinks and all. She resisted the urge. Reporters could be on the other side of that door and she didn't relish racking up a third nickname for herself.

"Thank you," she said, sweeping through ahead of him.

"Don't mention it."

"Mention it?" she tossed over her shoulder, thinking of a different method of revenge. "Funny you should say that. I was considering changing my speech today, making it more personal and anecdotal."

His footfall sounded right behind her. "Kate, I'm warning you—"

"After all, you told about the peanut jar," she said, returning the smiles of people sitting at round banquet tables covered with white linen and pink floral centerpieces. In the middle of the room stood an ice sculpture surrounded by more pink flowers. The sculpture resembled Rodin's classic work *The Kiss*. How well she remembered Garth's kiss, sizzling enough to melt that sculpture in a second.

"Listen, Kate, I—"

"Oh, waiter," someone called as they passed. "We don't have any water at this table."

"Better do your job," Kate said, and continued on up to the head table while savoring her small triumph. Garth didn't know that she'd never reveal what had happened between them. After what he'd done today, he could darn well sweat it out, though. Served him right.

The rectangular head table was elevated and held a tabletop lectern equipped with a microphone, a long, low centerpiece of pink chrysanthemums and baby's breath, and name cards for Kate and Melanie Exeter, owner of the La Jolla Book Bag. Kate had met her earlier that morning, before the autographing session. Melanie was already there, looking through the notes she would use to introduce Kate.

Mounting the two steps to the draped wooden platform, Kate felt the weight of all the attention in the room on her. Garth was down there, too. He'd be serving water and checking table settings, preparing the way for the lunch that would follow her short speech. And worrying.

As the scent of chrysanthemums assailed her, Kate took a deep breath and tried to slow her heartbeat. She chatted with Melanie and promptly forgot what she had said as soon as she'd said it. Her hands trembled; her palms were damp.

Melanie smiled at her. "Ready?"

Kate nodded. While Melanie gave the introduction, Kate glanced around the room, searching for Garth. He wasn't there, but Boz was, his head bandaged. He, too, wore a white pleated shirt, black bow tie, cummerbund and slacks. He had a carafe of coffee in each hand.

Boz. Maybe Garth hadn't told the press about the peanut jar. Maybe Boz had told them. Guilt pricked Kate; she'd accused Garth without knowing all the facts. Garth wouldn't have thrown the blame back on his friend, even if Boz had been responsible. Of course, Garth could still be the blabbermouth. Yet the more she thought about it, the more she suspected Boz.

Melanie finished, and Kate walked to the podium as the audience applauded, adding to the roaring sound in her ears. She adjusted the microphone, cleared her throat. "Good afternoon." She still wasn't used to hearing her voice projected out over a crowd. The voice didn't sound like hers, and yet it had to be. The people waited, their faces upturned, their eyes bright with expectation.

Kate glanced at her notes and began the prepared speech she'd given numerous times before. Stella had helped her create it. It was full of sexual facts and fantasies that always held a crowd spellbound. Kate felt the speech was bogus. The content represented only a small part of her book, the most sensational part detailing men's and women's differing sexual responses. She discussed numbers of climaxes, the difference in erogenous zones, even the fact that men fall into a narcoleptic state after sex while women want to cuddle. With Garth out there she had trouble with parts of the speech and feared she was blushing, but the audience seemed unaware of her discomfort and laughed at all the right moments.

She stopped to take a swallow of water from a goblet beside the lectern. In the back of the room Garth stood holding a pitcher of ice water. He was as still as the frozen man in the ice sculpture. This would be the perfect moment for her to reveal their relationship, she thought, knowing she'd never do it.

Kate looked back at her notes. She hated this speech. Really hated it. Stella wasn't here today. This was her last chance to speak to an audience, unless she counted the talk show a week from now. Kate knew she'd feel even less composed in front of television cameras.

No, now was the time to put a little of herself into all the hype. She'd been pandering to the "sex expert" image her publisher had created long enough. She stared down at her clasped hands, gathered her courage, and began. "Some of you have read my book and some of you haven't. But whether you've read it or not, all of you have expected something very specific from the title. I'd like to say something about that title. I didn't choose it, I don't like it, and I don't think it accurately represents what's in the book...or my personal style regarding my own relationships."

There was a murmur of surprise from the crowd, but she plunged on, not daring to look to see if Garth had stayed to hear this.

"The title implies that a woman must snag a man and then proceed to 'get' what she needs from him in the way of sex. The title implies manipulation. That's not what I advocate. My interviews with women and my own personal experiences tell me that manipulating others to behave the way you want is not the answer. The process of being happy in your relationship begins much earlier, when you first choose your partner. That choice must be made very carefully."

She found the courage to glance toward the back of the room. Garth was still there, his posture unchanged. He seemed transfixed by what she was saying.

"The qualities I think women should seek in a partner are honesty, integrity, shared values and a sense of humor," she continued, looking straight at him now. "Sex may bring you together, but it won't keep you together without the other important ingredients of a good relationship. In other words, to 'get the sex you need from your man,' as the title of the book says, you must first choose the right man. That's the main message of my book."

Garth took a step forward, as if he meant to stride right up to the podium, but then he stopped, as if suddenly aware of where he was. Kate realized with a jolt that she believed in Garth's honesty and integrity. Suddenly she knew for certain that he hadn't told the reporters about the peanut jar, nor had he been willing to rat on his friend. He also had a sense of humor, but as for shared values? There was the rub.

"If you are already in a relationship with a man who doesn't have all the qualities you treasure, you may be able to nurture the development of those qualities," she said. Did she really believe that? "And you may not," she added. "If not, there's no way in the world to 'get the sex you need,' or the love, either. And let me say something about that."

She couldn't look at Garth anymore. Had love played any part in their interaction? She had an aching feeling that it might have with her, and that spelled trouble. She forced herself to continue her speech. "This may be an old-fashioned view, but I don't view sex—good sex—as simply the mating of body parts. I believe that women, and I hope men, need more than that. Getting the sex you need won't happen unless, paired with that, you get the love you need. And again, you must look for certain qualities in a man before you can expect that kind of love. Don't be fooled by flash and dash. Pay attention to the inner person. Listen to him. See if he listens to you."

She paused again. Someone coughed, but other than that, the room was completely still. No one even rattled so much as a coffee cup. Kate's heart beat like a trip hammer. "I'd like to leave you with this thought, clichéd though it may be. Don't judge a book by its cover."

She sat down as the group applauded, some vociferously and others uncertainly. Garth no longer stood in the back of the room. He, along with the other waiters, were busy serving the first course, a tossed salad and hot rolls.

"That was very interesting," Melanie said, turning toward Kate.

"I don't think my publisher will like it much," she said. She discovered she was shaking. "Fortunately this is the last stop on the tour. As you may have guessed, I'm really ready to go home."

"I guessed," Melanie said, moving aside slightly so a waiter could place a salad in front of her. "Well, at least try to enjoy your meal. The food is still good here, although rumor has it the rest of the place is deteriorating."

"The food *is* good," Kate said, remembering her meal from the night before—remembering how Garth had come in, making fun of his abilities as a waiter. Then the candlelight, the wine, the feeling of intimacy.... The waiter set a plate of tossed greens and cleverly sliced vegetables in front of her.

He leaned down with a basket in his hand. "Hot roll, Dr. Kate?"

Kate wondered if the double entendre had been intentional; she *had* detected a slightly impertinent tone in the waiter's voice. She glanced up at the sandy-haired man as he set the basket on the table. Something about the way he returned her look made a chill run up her spine. Nervous reaction, she decided, and reached for a roll as he climbed back down the steps to the banquet floor. A piece of paper was stuck between the rolls, folded like a note.

Melanie noticed the paper, too. "Someone hiding a note in the rolls?" she asked with a laugh. "How inventive and romantic. An admirer?"

For one wild moment Kate thought perhaps Garth had done it. She unfolded the paper and started at the message scrawled there. Dropping it on the table, she leapt up and stumbled down the steps as she tried to see which way the waiter had gone. This couldn't be happening. The nightmare was supposed to be over when she left here.

Get a dog, the policeman had said earlier. Panic squeezed her heart as she stumbled between the tables, trying to find the waiter. The words of the note played over and over in her mind. "See you in Nebraska."

10

THE FIRST PERSON she found was Boz, not Garth. She grabbed his arm, nearly making him spill the coffee he carried. "That man was here," she said in an undertone, continuing to scan the room. People were staring at her, but she couldn't help that. "He's working as a waiter."

"You mean that guy who—"

"Yes. Where's Garth?"

"In the kitchen. Come on." Still carrying both carafes of coffee, Boz led her through the maze of tables and out the room via the swinging double doors. "He was working as a waiter? Did you recognize him?"

"In a way." Kate watched as two waiters passed them in the hall. Neither was the man who had served her the hot rolls. She and Boz pushed through aluminum doors into the steamy kitchen.

"Garth?" Boz set down the coffee as he called across to a far counter where Garth was loading up a tray with salad plates.

He turned immediately, took one look at Kate and directed the nearest person to finish the job. "What is it?" he asked, hurrying over.

At that moment, gazing at the solid strength of him, the concern in his gray eyes, she was grateful to have him as an ally, no matter what his sexual politics were. "The man who broke into my room last night is here, working as a waiter," she said.

"Damn!" Garth glanced at Boz. "Notify security and call the police. Tell them to look for—" He turned back to Kate. "Did you see his face this time?"

"Sort of." Her pulse was racing. "He left a note in the basket of hot rolls, telling me he'd see me in Nebraska. After I read the note I realized his voice had sounded familiar, but by then he was gone. All I remember is the sandy hair, which we knew from before, and kind of a hooked nose."

Garth blanched. "I hired somebody with sandy hair and a hooked nose this morning when we were so short-handed. That son of a bitch. Okay, Boz. Tell them to look for a guy about five-nine, with sandy hair cut short, a hooked nose, heavy eyebrows, and . . . and what?" He paused and stared at the ceiling. "Dammit, why can't I remember more?"

"That's good enough," Boz said, starting out of the kitchen.

"And a mole," Garth called after him. "On the side of his nose."

"Got it." Boz pushed through the door.

"Come on." Garth took Kate's hand and pulled her toward the outside kitchen door. "Let's take a tour of our own. We're the two people who'll recognize him first."

They stepped into brilliant sunshine that made Kate's eyes water. The clouds that had brought rain early that morning had scudded out to sea, leaving a clear blue sky and warm sun.

"Maybe we should split up," she said. "I'll go one way and you the other. We can meet back here."

"Not a chance." He held her hand firmly as he hurried down a walkway leading to the beach. "That jerk would probably love to catch you wandering around by yourself."

"Don't think I'm just some helpless—"

"I'm well aware that you're not helpless." He stopped and checked up and down the beach, his eyes crinkling as he squinted against the sun. "But I'm not risking this hotel's reputation so that you can prove it to the world."

She pulled her hand from his. "So it's the hotel's reputation you're worried about, and not my safety?"

"What difference does it make? They come out to the same thing."

"Not in the least, and you know it."

He glanced down at her. "What do you want me to say?"

That this morning meant something to you. "Nothing," she said.

"I didn't think so. Let's walk down to the end of the units and go around the side. This is probably a wild-goose chase. I'll bet he's miles away from here by now, but we may as well keep looking." He moved onto the sand.

"Let me take off my shoes." She stepped out of her pink pumps and picked them up while he waited. "Okay." The sand warmed her stockinged feet and brought a murmur of pleasure. She wriggled her toes and felt some of her tension ease. Her first chance to walk on the beach, and she had to be chasing some creep; the unfairness of it assailed her again.

They trudged along without speaking, Garth's shoes crunching against the sand, Kate's stocking-clad feet making a sibilant whisper. She studied every man she saw, but her scrutiny yielded only a middle-aged jogger with his golden retriever, a father playing with his baby under an umbrella stuck in the sand, and a hotel employee, a dark-haired, dark-skinned fellow raking up seaweed on the beach.

Gulls glided overhead and sandpipers looking like windup toys skittered through the retreating waves at the waterline. Kate breathed in the combined fragrances of salt water, warm sand and suntan lotion. The man they sought was gone; she could feel it.

"No sign of him," Garth said, pausing to look behind them and ahead down the beach toward the Scripps' pier.

"No." Kate stopped and shaded her eyes against the sun. Not a single sandy-haired man in sight.

"What did he say in the note again?"

"That he'd see me in Nebraska. I guess he's not giving up." Kate took off her white jacket and slung it over her shoulder.

"What sort of protection do you have there in Nebraska?"

She laughed. "Are you kidding? It's a little college town. People forget to lock their doors, let alone remember to put in alarm systems. As for the cop's idea about a dog, I'm renting my house and I think there's a rule against pets."

"Could you stay with friends, or maybe have someone stay there with you?"

She considered the possibility. She could stay with Donna, but Donna smoked. Kate didn't mind as long as she didn't have to live with her. Jennie's little efficiency apartment would cramp them horribly, and Ann was living with Gil, so that was out. "I can't think of anybody," she said.

"Parents? Brothers or sisters?"

"My dad's dead, and I couldn't last two days living with my mother. My sister has a big family in a small house, a job and a demanding husband." Kate shook her head. "No real help there. I could move to a place that allows dogs, but not in a week, which is what I have between now and the talk show in L.A. next Saturday."

Garth rubbed his chin and frowned.

"Maybe the police will catch him today," she suggested.

"I doubt it."

Kate sighed. She wanted so much to forget this mess. Why couldn't she comb the beach for shells and dabble her toes in the water? Why couldn't she smooth coconut-scented suntan lotion on herself and stretch out on a beach towel to read a book? Nothing scholarly or deep like she usually read, but a paperback novel with lots of adventure and romance in it.

She glanced sideways at Garth. As long as she was fantasizing, she'd add him to the picture, put him on a beach towel next to hers, reading...her book. She sighed again, but this time with disappointment. Then she whirled to face the ocean and spread out her arms. "This is so blasted unfair! Here I am on a beautiful beach that I can't enjoy, and I'm going home to a peaceful town where I won't be safe. All because some sociopath has singled me out. I want my life back! I want to be able to play on the beach, walk down a street, eat a meal without looking over my shoulder. Is that so much to ask?"

"It is if you're Dr. Kate."

She turned back to find him watching her, his hands in his pockets, an unreadable expression on his face. Sometime during their walk he'd taken off his bow tie and unfastened the top few buttons of his tuxedo shirt. Dark chest hair curled from the open shirt, reminding her of what that curling hair had felt like against her skin. "I wish Dr. Kate would just disappear," she said.

He studied her a while longer. "Maybe that could be arranged."

"How?"

He started to speak and then shook his head. "Never mind. It's a stupid idea. You should probably go home and get a security service to watch your house."

"Probably, but tell me what you were thinking, anyway."

"It must be Boz's influence. I haven't thought up stunts like this since we were in college."

"Are you going to tell me or not?"

He shrugged. "I guess, just to give you a laugh. What I was thinking is that you could head out to the airport in the limo, as if you were leaving, to make your stalker friend think you were really going back to Nebraska. Then at the airport you could disguise yourself in the

bathroom and come back here under an assumed name."
He shot her a wry smile. "Pretty ridiculous, huh?"

Her heart began to thud faster. Was it possible that he
wanted her to stay? "Maybe not so ridiculous. What sort
of disguise? And how would I get hold of one?"

"Oh, that part's easy. Boz loves stuff like that. We
could send him to buy a wig and some different clothes,
a wild pair of sunglasses. He'd have a ball."

Kate allowed herself to imagine it. She wouldn't have
to leave this paradise by the sea just yet. She wouldn't
have to leave Garth. Of course, they probably had no
future together, but then again, he was the one suggesting she hang around a few more days. A disguise. It was
a crazy idea, but they'd run out of conventional ones....

Then a brilliant strategy for determining Garth's mo-
tives struck her. "So I'd be staying here?"

"That was the idea."

"I can't afford it, Garth. My publisher's paid for everything so far. My advance on the book wasn't very big,
and I won't get any royalties until—"

"I'll cover the expense."

She stared at him. He *did* want her to stay. "Why?"

His gaze flicked away. "I'm not completely sure of the
answer to that. Part of it is that I think you deserve a
break. I'm beginning to understand that you didn't want
or expect this circus when you wrote your book."

"That's right," she said softly. Maybe, just maybe, he
was coming around.

"And even if the disguise thing doesn't work, at least
you'll be around a lot of people while you're staying at

the Pelican. If you go back to Nebraska, you'll be pretty much on your own."

"That's true." *And I wouldn't have you to protect me.*

His gaze returned to hers and he took a step closer. "So that's part of the reason, but not all of it. While you were making your speech, I...thought about some things and realized I didn't want you to fly back to Nebraska this afternoon. But that seemed inevitable, so I told myself to forget about you."

A lump formed in her throat. Their lovemaking had been important for him, too. She'd been right. This man didn't think of women in terms of conquests. He cared about her. "Garth—"

"Not that I could have easily forgotten you." He moved closer, near enough to touch her cheek. The expression in his gray eyes grew soft; tenderness transformed the stern lines around his mouth. "But I was going to try. Now, with the way things are, maybe this idea would buy us a little time. I think we could use that."

"So do I." She could barely form the words. Her chest was tight with the excitement of knowing that he cared enough to ask her to stay.

"We need time for this." He leaned down and brushed his lips against hers.

She closed her eyes and he continued the caress with firmer pressure. Then with a groan he swept her into his arms. Her jacket fell to the sand as she surrendered to the power of his kiss. Her senses reeled from the warmth of the sun, the sound of the waves and this man wanting her, needing what she could give. Perhaps fantasies came true, after all.

Still holding her tight, he lifted his head. "If any reporters wander out here, our goose is cooked."

"They should be gone. They got copies of my speech, so they wouldn't have stayed for it."

"Some speech."

She hesitated. "You liked it, didn't you?"

"Very much."

She sighed with relief. They had a real chance. "Then I guess I'll stay."

"I was prepared to kiss you until you said you would."

"Then maybe I haven't made up my mind."

He leaned down, but she laughed and placed her finger against his mouth. "I'm staying, Garth. And we're really being foolish, doing this in full view of anyone who cares to stroll by. We should go back."

He kissed her finger. "Don't want to."

"The sooner I finish with my responsibilities, the sooner I can come back as some stranger who is free to do whatever she likes."

His hold on her tightened. "I like that idea."

"Do you really think Boz can make me look like someone else?"

Garth chuckled, and for the first time Kate imagined what he might have been like as a devil-may-care college student, back when he and Boz met. "I have absolutely no doubt about it," he said, smiling down at her. "In fact, he'll probably want to get into the act himself, if I know Boz."

THREE HOURS LATER, as Kate carried her disguise in a shopping bag toward the airport rest room, she reflected that Garth knew Boz very well, indeed. He had leapt on the plan and added his own embellishments, namely that he would disguise himself, drive separately to the airport, and then he and Kate would arrive at the Pelican as "Mr. and Mrs. Hannibal Throckmorton from Des Moines."

A line of women trailed out from the rest room. A flight must have just landed, Kate thought, grimacing. Then her impatience changed to gratitude. A crowded rest room would confuse her pursuer if he lost track of who had gone in and who had come out. At last she worked her way inside the door and soon after was able to take the shopping bag containing her disguise into a stall. She'd checked her bags to maintain the subterfuge, but she'd left some of her clothes and toiletries back in Garth's room.

The past three hours had been hectic. Kate and Garth had given the police a revised description of the man they were seeking, and the police had said they'd notify airport security to be on the lookout for someone matching that description. By then the luncheon had ended and Kate had hurriedly autographed a few more books before going back to her room to pack. She hadn't had time to call her mother or Stella to alert them to her change of plans, but she'd do that once she returned to the Pelican. *And Garth.*

Undressing in the tiny bathroom stall, Kate felt as if she were shedding her identity of the past ten days. She'd been furious with Garth when he'd suggested that she was really two people. Maybe she'd been furious because that was the way she herself had felt—dishonest in the way she'd presented herself. Garth's comment might have hit a nerve.

Kate stepped out of her pink shoes and stripped off her panty hose. The tile was cold on her bare feet, but she comforted herself by thinking of the warm sand at the Pelican. *Warm sand, warm arms, warm lips...* who was she kidding? The beach would be nice, but she was really rushing back to Garth.

She pulled her disguise out of the shopping bag. Boz had chosen white shorts, a purple tank top cut too skimpily for a bra, sandals, a Dolly Parton wig and enormous purple sunglasses. Kate chuckled to herself as she donned the outfit. She might have predicted something like this. Boz wouldn't have tried to disguise her as some dowdy, sexless woman—it wasn't his style. The wig took a little doing. She shoved her own hair under the webbed cap and adjusted it with the help of a mirror in her purse. The whole exercise reminded her of grade school Halloween parties, when kids put on their costumes in the bathroom during recess.

At the bottom of the shopping bag was a lightweight zippered tote. Kate folded her clothes and packed them inside, along with her purse and shoes. Nothing about her was supposed to look the same when she emerged from the rest room. Taking the purple sunglasses in one hand, she unlatched the stall door and stepped outside. Glancing in the wide mirror over the row of sinks, she gasped and did a double take.

She no longer looked like Dr. Kate, but she didn't much resemble Kate Newberry, college professor, either. She looked exactly like a free-spirited woman anticipating a sexy vacation on the beach. She wondered if she would be able to forget the book tour, forget the man following her, and become the person she saw in the mirror. With one last look at the blond bombshell she'd become, she shouldered the canvas tote and left the rest room.

Boz had told her he'd be wearing a blond handlebar mustache and a legionnaire's hat to hide the bandage on the back of his head. She spotted him immediately. He'd added a loud Hawaiian shirt and had a camera around his neck. As she walked toward him, she tried not to laugh. "Why, Hannibal, there you are," she said, laying a hand on his arm.

"Leticia, how wonderful you look," he said, his blue eyes dancing. "I can hardly wait for you to meet my friend Garth Fredericks."

Kate felt her cheeks grow warm. "This outfit is darned skimpy, Hannibal."

"Yeah, I know. I was thinking of Garth." His mustache tilted as he grinned and guided her toward the exit.

So was Kate. She hadn't worn clothes this free moving since high school, and the feeling was liberating. Had she really become so stodgy? Kate realized that in one sense the woman returning to the Pelican with Boz really wasn't the same one who had left the resort not long ago.

"Any sign of our friend with the hooked nose and the mole?" Boz asked as they wended their way through the crowd.

"Not that I've seen. I'm glad you're here, though. I've been a little jumpy, wondering if he'd turn up."

"But the chauffeur stayed with you until you left for the rest room, right?"

"Yes."

"That's good. Garth would have had his hide if he hadn't."

Kate felt a warm glow of satisfaction at the evidence of Garth's protectiveness toward her. "I wonder if we fooled the guy."

Boz glanced down at her. "I don't know, but you sure don't look like the same woman to me. Good thing I warned Garth, or he might not even recognize you."

Kate smiled. "You know, Boz, this is kind of fun."

Boz looked pleased. "I told Garth we had you figured wrong."

"And how did you have me figured?" Kate asked, although she thought she knew.

"Just...different," Boz said, and held the door for her as they walked outside the terminal.

Sometime later they left the airport in a rented Ford Taurus, and Kate leaned back against the seat with relief. "I think we made it."

"One more hurdle. The front desk at the Pelican."

"Don't you think they'll recognize you, Boz?"

"You'd think so, but probably not. We have a fairly high turnover of desk personnel, and besides, they see so many people in the course of a day they don't notice individual appearances that much."

Kate considered his comment about a high turnover and remembered her earlier suspicion that Boz wasn't running the resort as well as Garth had hoped. Boz hadn't looked much like the manager of a top-notch resort when she'd first glimpsed him through the peephole in her door. If he had looked more official, she might not have clobbered him with the peanut jar. She still winced whenever she thought about that. "How's your head?" she asked, glancing at him.

"Okay." He looked uncomfortable. "By the way, I'm sorry about telling that story to the press. Garth tried to stop me, but I just plowed right in, as usual."

"Oh, well." Kate found it difficult to get mad at Boz. He seemed to have such a good heart, and he'd been so glad to help her with this escape plan. "I guess maybe we're even. I feel terrible about hitting you over the head."

"Don't worry about that." He grimaced. "I could use a little whack on the head now and then."

She studied him a moment. "Are you always so hard on yourself?" In the pause that followed, she thought he wasn't going to answer, but finally he sighed and settled back in his seat.

"He shouldn't have given me this manager's job," he said, his voice bleak.

"You mean Garth?"

"Yeah. Mr. Perfect. He's never made a false move in his life. Don't get me wrong. I admire the hell out of the guy, and he's been a real pal to me, but I learned a long time ago that I couldn't hang with him when it came to business deals and money. Garth just doesn't make mistakes." He paused. "Unless you count his hiring me to manage the Pelican."

Kate's heart went out to him. "Oh, Boz, it can't be that bad. Running a resort must be complicated, and in time you'll—"

"Not too complicated for Garth. He could do it with one hand tied behind his back. Me—I'm too easygoing. When I make decisions, they're usually the wrong ones.

In the beginning I thought I could handle this job. In fact, I thought I was doing pretty good, although we weren't showing much of a profit, but I blamed that on the economy. Now that Garth's here I see things through his eyes. It's not just the economy. I've really screwed the place up."

Kate tried to think of something, anything to say that would ease Boz's pain. "Garth can't be that perfect," she said gently. "After all, his marriage didn't work out."

"That wasn't his fault. Judith killed the whole thing. Got a whole bunch of those damned self-help books and started telling Garth how miserable their marriage was. They'd still be married except for those crazy books. They—" He stopped speaking and looked at her. Slowly a dark red flush crept up his neck. "Well, that was typical of the Boz. Put my foot right in it again."

Kate felt as if someone had just ripped a curtain aside to show her a previously hidden view. So Garth's wife had wielded self-help books as a weapon in their marital disputes. That explained a lot. It also sent a question skittering across her mind. She didn't want to think about it, but she was a scientist of human behavior. She could no more ignore questions than stop breathing. If Garth hated self-help books because he believed they'd ruined his marriage, then he apparently regretted the divorce. If he regretted the divorce . . . he might still love his wife.

11

"LOOK, THAT WAS STUPID," Boz said, his face glowing with embarrassment.

"It's okay," Kate said, even though it wasn't. Her mind kept nudging up against the possibility that Garth still loved his wife. If he did, Kate wouldn't be able to avoid the hurt.

"No, it's not okay," Boz insisted. "In the first place, I insulted you, and in the second, I shouldn't be babbling about Garth's marriage. It's none of my business."

"Please, don't apologize." Kate stared ahead at the traffic as they whizzed along the freeway toward La Jolla. "You've probably kept me from making a big mistake."

"I don't like the sound of that."

"No, really, Boz. I'm glad to know more about the breakup of Garth's marriage. I think it's important that I do."

"Oh, great. Boy, I've really loused things up, haven't I?"

"You've clarified things. And I appreciate it."

"Listen, Garth might not be crazy about the book you wrote, but I can tell he really likes you." Boz stumbled on, seeming determined to fix the problem. "I mean, you can see how he'd feel, if books like yours . . . well, maybe not exactly like yours, but books similar to yours have—"

"Certainly," Kate cut in, unable to listen to any more. "I'm really glad to know about this, Boz. And everything will be fine. Don't worry. Let's not talk about it anymore, okay?"

"You're holding it against him," Boz said miserably. "I can tell by your tone of voice. Here I am bringing you back to Garth, and I've made you upset with him. Maybe I should just go out and shoot myself."

That forced a sad chuckle out of Kate. "Maybe you should save a bullet for me."

GARTH PACED the lobby, impatient for Boz and Kate to return. He'd officially checked out of his suite and into a room on the same floor. He'd taken all Kate's belongings with him into the other room, so the maid could get the suite ready for the Throckmortons from Des Moines. He'd already told anyone within earshot that he was a close personal friend of Mrs. Throckmorton. Garth didn't expect to use the second room for anything but a decoy. If things went as planned, he'd spend the week with Kate in that suite, in that king-size bed.

He'd notified his secretary in Boston that he'd be staying on at the Pelican for a few more days. She'd seemed delighted. Apparently he hadn't been much fun around the office the past few months. She'd promised to keep him up to date and fax him any crucial correspondence or market news, but for the first time in many years, Garth found himself uninterested in the fate of his investments. In the lobby he'd picked up a *Wall Street*

Journal and thrown it down again within a few minutes. His attention was completely focused on Kate Newberry. What had Boz dreamed up as her fake name? Leticia? He'd have to remember to call her that in public. After all, he was a close personal friend. Very close.

A Ford Taurus pulled into the circular driveway and Timothy stepped forward to open the passenger door. A dynamite blonde stepped out, the type that looked fantastic in just the sort of skimpy outfit she had on. Garth looked closer and his heart hammered. He knew those legs, the curve of that chin. His mouth went dry. He'd known she had a wonderful body, but he'd never had quite this perspective on it before. Timothy was surreptitiously ogling and Garth wanted to punch him out. He also wanted to grab Kate and bundle her up to the suite.

Timothy held the door and Kate breezed in, followed by Boz in his handlebar mustache.

Garth stepped forward. "Leticia," he boomed, reaching for her hands. "How good to see you." Her hands were like ice and he couldn't see her eyes behind the purple sunglasses. Fear washed over him as he wondered if she'd been followed by the sandy-haired man, after all. "Everything all right?" he murmured as he brushed his cheek against hers.

"Fine," she said. Her smile seemed forced.

Something was wrong, but he wouldn't be able to find out what until he paid her a visit later. He released her hands and turned to Boz. "Hannibal, you old bastard, how are you? How's Des Moines?"

"Same as ever," Boz said, looking worried.

"Any trouble with the flight?" Garth asked, desperate for some hint of what the problem was.

"Not a bit," Boz said. "Except the airline lost the luggage."

Garth expressed dismay, although they'd worked this out in advance so they wouldn't have to fool with decoy suitcases, too.

"What the heck?" Boz said. "Who needs clothes?"

"You have a point," Garth said, glancing at Kate to see if she'd respond with a smile, a look, anything to tell him she'd picked up on the joke. Nothing. She still hadn't taken off the damned sunglasses. It was a wonder she didn't stumble over the furniture as they walked toward the check-in desk. He stayed nearby as Boz signed the registration forms; Garth told the clerk not to worry about getting a credit card imprint, that all expenses were to be charged to his account.

"Say, Garth," Boz said as a bellman came over to show them up to the suite, "after we get settled I'll meet you in the lounge for a drink. Leticia wants to rest, I think."

Garth frowned. That wasn't the way he'd planned for things to go. He'd expected Boz to clear out and leave the room to him and Kate. "Sure," he said, smiling and clapping Boz on the back. "We'll catch up on old times."

"Right." Boz looked nervous. Kate looked like an icicle. Garth couldn't figure any of it, but he was sure he'd get an explanation soon. He headed off to the lounge to wait.

Less than ten minutes later, right after Garth had been served a cup of coffee, Boz came into the lounge, still wearing his legionnaire hat. The plan was that sometime tonight Hannibal Throckmorton would be called back to Des Moines on business but Mrs. Throckmorton would stay on to enjoy the pleasures of the Pelican. Garth had hoped to be one of them. Now he wasn't so sure.

"I messed it up for you," Boz said as he collapsed into a barrel chair across from Garth. "I let it slip that Judith used those self-help books against you, that they helped break you guys up and that was why you hated them so much."

Garth stared across at Boz, who looked like a sad-eyed Scottie in his mustache and crazy hat. Garth blew out a breath. "I guess I should be glad it was that and not the guy with the hooked nose. I thought maybe he'd made another appearance or something."

Boz shook his head. "That's what makes me so mad at myself. This deal was going smooth as silk. I think we fooled the jerk, and she seemed real happy, like she was anticipating coming back here, you know?"

Garth thought of the heightened feelings he himself had felt over the past hour. "I know."

"Anyway, when I told her, she got quiet and said she was glad I'd told her, that it had kept her from making a big mistake."

"Damn."

"I'm sorry, Gartho. God, do you want me to go to the bookstore and get you one of her books? Maybe if you read it and told her it was great, she'd—"

"I'm not going to read some damned book before I talk to her," Garth said, pushing back his chair. "In fact, I refuse to let that book stand between us. Is she in the suite?"

"Far as I know."

"Then I think I'll pay Leticia Throckmorton a visit." Garth left the lounge and headed for the fire stairs. In his frame of mind he didn't want to wait for an elevator. He took the stairs two at a time while he tried to figure out why Boz's revelation should have changed the climate so much between Kate and him. She already knew he didn't like self-help books. If anything, she should be more understanding now that she'd been given a reason. Wasn't that what psychologists were supposed to do best? Understand?

On the second floor he headed for her door and rapped on it. He drummed his fingers against his thigh while he waited, imagining her studying him through the peephole. What if she wouldn't let him in? At last the door swung open and she stood there, minus the wig but still dressed in the purple tank top and white shorts. Her feet were bare.

At the sight of her, his breath caught and he forgot everything he'd meant to say. Memories of their lovemaking assaulted him, stirring smoldering desire into a hot flame. But the expression on her face was closed, forbidding. He swallowed. "May I come in?"

She seemed to consider it for a moment before stepping back and allowing him to enter.

He closed the door behind him and turned to her. "Boz told me about your conversation on the way back from the airport."

"Yes, he was very enlightening."

How he wanted to kiss her, but some instinct warned him to keep his arms at his sides. "Obviously what he said has made a difference to you."

She nodded.

"Kate, I don't get it. You knew before that I had a prejudice against the kind of books you write. You seemed to have . . . accepted it, somehow, after what happened last night. But now . . ." He spread his hands in frustration.

She folded her arms. "Tell me, Garth, how do you feel about your ex-wife?"

"Judith?" He paused in confusion. This wasn't the question he'd expected. He wondered if it was a trick one. Maybe she'd concluded that he hated women or something.

"Let's put it another way. Let's imagine that Judith told you that she never should have read all those books and that she still loved you and wanted a reconciliation. What would you do?"

He felt like a bug under a microscope. No doubt about it, she was watching him very closely. He thought about her question, and realized the idea of Judith wanting to have him back generated no feelings in him whatsoever. Well, maybe pity for Judith, but that was about all. He shrugged. "I guess I might feel sorry for her."

"*Sorry* for her?"

He decided that was the wrong answer. "Okay, how about concerned? Wishing she'd find somebody else? Hell, Kate, what do you want me to say?"

Her expression softened and she stepped forward. "I think you just said it."

"Lady, you aren't making a damn bit of sense." But his heart quickened at the look in her eyes. If she'd been frozen before, the thaw had begun.

"From your response, it seems I drew the wrong conclusion. But psychologically speaking, your intense dislike of self-help books could indicate that you're unhappy about the divorce, which logically led me to the conclusion that you still have a strong attraction, a love relationship, as it were, with your—"

"Good God." He groaned and hauled her into his arms. "I'll show you a strong attraction." He couldn't seem to hold her tight enough or close enough as he gazed into her upturned face. Early this morning, when he'd last touched her like this, seemed aeons ago.

"You don't love her anymore?" she whispered.

"No, I don't love her anymore. Do you think I could be this way with you if I still loved Judith?"

"Some men—"

"I'm not some men," he said, sliding both hands down to cup her bottom and align her precisely where he wanted her.

Her auburn eyebrows arched. "I'm beginning to understand that."

"And don't try to fit me into your charts and statistics. I won't go."

She wound both arms around his neck and snuggled her breasts in close, playing havoc with his breathing. Her eyes issued an invitation that made his heart hammer. "Then where do you fit, Mr. Fredericks?"

"I thought you'd never ask." He scooped her up and carried her into the bedroom. Still love Judith? What a laugh. How could he love Judith when he was rapidly falling in love with... The thought hit him like a semi and brought him to a halt.

Kate reached up and stroked his cheek. "Change your mind?"

He gazed down at her, this woman he'd known such a short time, this woman he wanted more than he wanted to keep breathing. She, with all her confounded psychology, would say what he was feeling wasn't possible. She'd have a fancy name for it, and use that name to describe her own reactions. She wouldn't believe herself in love with him. But he had a week. "No, I haven't changed my mind." Exactly the opposite. He kissed her hard before rolling with her onto the bed.

She laughed as they tumbled together, but the laugh was husky, tinged with her own need. He smiled down at her. "This is the sexiest outfit I've ever seen, but I want it off now."

She lifted her arms over her head. "So do I."

The gesture swept away any remaining restraint and turned his whole body into a heat-seeking missile. Her clothes came away as easily as tissue paper and he eagerly filled his hands and mouth with the lemon-scented wonder of her.

She was less inhibited with him this time, more willing to moan and whimper, to tell him how he pleased her. Beneath his fingers her nipples hardened and ripened for the flick of his tongue, the warm receptacle of his mouth. He stroked downward, his palms smoothing over her silken curves and searching out the moist wellspring of her passion. His kisses rained over her breasts, her stomach, her thighs. He explored the backs of her knees, her instep, even the spaces between her pink-polished toes. With each caress he celebrated the joy of having her back in his arms.

Somewhere in the frenzy of loving her he realized she'd been tugging at his clothes. He paused in his sensual assault to help her, suddenly aware of how much he needed her touch.

"You are so good to me," she murmured. Her voice had a sexy catch in it that told him her pulse was racing at the same speed as his. "Let me be good to you."

He quivered with anticipation as she kissed him with deceptive softness.

Then she lifted her head and gazed into his eyes as she rubbed her hands over his chest. "I love touching you," she whispered, moving one hand lower, across his belly.

He was breathing hard. "Go easy," he warned.

"I love the look in your eyes. The fire that leaps there when I do this."

He sighed. "Oh, Kate, you're—" when her fingers wrapped around his shaft, he thought the game would be over, but he clenched his teeth against the urge to explode, knowing that if he could hold on, he'd enjoy some of the greatest moments this side of heaven "—wonderful," he groaned.

"I can be even more wonderful."

His chin lifted with the effort to control himself as her mouth closed around him. The pleasure eclipsed every other sensation and the throbbing in his groin threatened to overcome his steel grip on his response. Grasping her shoulders, he pulled her back up and rolled her onto her back. "Enough," he gasped.

"We'll never have enough."

He stared at her. Did she realize what was happening to them, after all? "You're right," he said. He nearly pulled the bedside-table drawer from its moorings in his search for the cellophane package that would gain him entrance to paradise. He found the package and tore into it.

"Let me," she said, reaching for it.

"No. If you touch me there again I'm done for." He sheathed himself with trembling hands and came to her, his body damp with the strain of all that wanting. Eager and ready, she opened to him and he slid home, closing his eyes with ecstasy. He opened them to find her gaze filled with an emotion he'd call love, but she might not, so he stayed quiet. The moment was too good to spoil with words, anyway.

He watched passion widen her eyes, part her trembling lips. She murmured his name, soft as a benediction, then gasped as the moment of release neared. He reveled in this fusion, this perfect melding of bodies, and yes . . . souls.

He felt the shudder of her climax, saw it register in the depth of her eyes, and surrendered himself to the most explosive sexual release of his life. Through the haze as tremors shook him, he heard her call his name, and knew that this was the voice he was meant to hear for the rest of his life. Here, at last, was his mate. The last feeling he had before he dropped off to sleep was a sense of guardianship. He would see that no one harmed this woman. Not ever.

AT THE SAN DIEGO AIRPORT Eddie had watched until Dr. Kate had checked her bags and headed for the can. He'd hung around, waiting for her to come out again, but somehow in the crowd he must have missed her. Didn't matter, he thought. Might as well get a head start. Nebraska was a hell of a drive from California.

Too bad he couldn't fly there, like the bitch was about to do, but it cost too much, and besides, he'd need his truck for this. Near as he could tell, Northbluff wasn't even big enough for bus lines and taxis. Should be a lead-pipe cinch to find out where a big-shot author like Dr. Kate Newberry lived. He sure was glad somebody had thought to put something on the book cover to tell him where the bitch lived. He'd memorized the stuff about her:

> Kate Newberry, Ph.D., wrote *Getting the Sex You Need from Your Man* originally as a textbook to be used in a course she hopes to institute at Northbluff College in Nebraska, but her editors soon recognized that the book would appeal to the general public. "Dr. Kate," as she's rapidly becoming known, is a popular lecturer at Northbluff and the author of several articles published in professional journals. Although this is her first entry into the popular psychology arena, it can hardly be her last.

As he pointed his truck northeast, Eddie Gump vowed that it would be exactly that. Once he made Dr. Kate see the light, she wouldn't feel like writing anything except maybe grocery lists.

12

LYING BENEATH GARTH and listening to his even breathing, Kate wondered if she'd ever been this happy in her life. She hated to change a single thing about the moment, but she'd have to wake him up. His weight was beginning to squeeze the breath out of her.

Slowly she trailed a finger down his spine. He nuzzled his face against her neck and kept sleeping. She turned her head and murmured in his ear. "Garth, you're crushing me."

"Mmph."

"Garth, wake up. I can't breathe." She tried pushing at his chest, but he was like a rock against her. Finally she reached down and pinched his bottom.

With a yelp he rolled away from her, then regarded her with an injured expression. "Is that how you get rid of your lovers?"

She smiled and touched his cheek. "I was beginning to suffocate and you wouldn't wake up."

"Oh." His expression changed to chagrin. "Guess I was asleep. Not very romantic, huh?"

"But typical of many men, as you'd know if you listened to my speech. Research shows that a good deal of the time men fall asleep after sex. That's what causes some of the communication problems that women—"

"Whoa." He caught her chin in his hand. "I heard your speech, Dr. Newberry. Let's talk about Garth and Kate. Did I insult you by falling asleep?"

"No, because I understand that it's a natural reaction to—"

"One of the most satisfying experiences of my life," he murmured. "And I shouldn't have let myself fall asleep before telling you so. You're wonderful, Kate." He kissed her lightly on the lips.

"So are you." She gazed into his eyes and her heart swelled as she read the depth of feeling there.

"I certainly didn't want to fall asleep, but I was awake most of last night, and I guess it caught up with me."

"The love seat was too small?"

"No, too close." He tickled her nose. "To you. Now if you'll excuse me, I have to leave this cozy spot for a minute." He headed for the bathroom. "Don't go away."

"I wouldn't dream of it." She dreamed of other things while he was gone, however, such as how delicious the next few days would be, now that she knew Garth wasn't still emotionally involved with his ex-wife. Kate stretched and nudged back the sheets so she could crawl under them. The light filtering through a crack in the closed drapes was muted; the sun must be sinking toward the sea, she thought. Maybe, if she put on her wig, she and Garth could take a walk along the beach at sunset.

"You look happy," Garth said as he returned from the bathroom and pulled the sheet back to slip in beside her. "And sexy as hell," he added, gathering her close.

She nestled against him. "I was thinking we might get dressed and take a sunset walk along the beach." The warmth and excitement of holding him close made the prospect less appealing than it had been a few moments earlier.

"I have nothing against walking." He stroked her hair. "But the getting dressed part sounds like a real drag."

"Yeah. Let's forget it." Snuggling closer, she marveled at how relaxed, yet completely alert she felt. Like a touch lamp, she began to glow with the slightest pressure of his fingers.

"Speaking of clothes, that was some outfit Boz picked out for you." Garth began a lazy massage of her back.

"I haven't worn anything like that since I was in high school." She wondered how a man's caress could feel so comforting, yet exciting at the same time.

"You looked great." He sighed and leaned down to kiss her lips gently. "Trust the Boz to dress you up so that I was practically salivating when you walked into the lobby."

"He was trying to please you, I think." She rubbed her finger against the cleft in his chin. "Did you know he thinks you're just about perfect?"

Garth chuckled. "He was putting you on. Boz doesn't—"

"Oh, yes, he does," Kate interrupted. "In fact, I think you intimidate him."

"I intimidate Boz?" Garth drew away slightly and stared down at her. "Come on. We've known each other for over twenty years."

"During which time you've become very successful and he hasn't. He says you don't make mistakes."

"That's ridiculous. Of course I make mistakes."

"Maybe you should tell Boz that."

Although Garth didn't move, Kate felt him mentally back away from her. She'd have to be pretty dim not to understand the reason. He reacted this way whenever she started talking like a psychologist. But she was a professional, dammit, and he needed help with this relationship! She gazed at his now-stony expression. "Obviously you don't appreciate my comments."

"It's just that you sound remarkably like the marriage counselor Judith dragged me to. This psychologist type said I come off as some kind of superman, and that I needed to become vulnerable, to 'open up,' as the trite phrase goes." His jaw clenched.

"Sometimes the phrase fits," she said gently.

"I couldn't say, but I can say that I'm sick of hearing it. Do you think I've made a success of myself in the business world by being vulnerable?"

Kate swallowed. This wasn't going well, but if she backed down now, she'd have to back down every time he challenged her. "No one's asking you to bare your soul to the world, Garth, but admitting mistakes to those you care about is what makes us all human."

Garth turned away from her and sat up, swinging his legs to the floor. "I think I just proved how human I am. I wanted you so much just now that I..." He combed his fingers through his hair. "Oh, what's the use? You have me all figured out, don't you?"

Kate's heart ached. Paradise had a snake in it, after all. "I guess I don't have you figured out," she murmured. "I'd never have guessed you'd be so defensive."

"Defensive," he muttered, and reached for his clothes. "There's another one of those workhorse words of your profession. Let anybody get upset with your diagnosis and they're labeled 'defensive.'"

"Garth, I was only trying—"

"To tell me how to deal with a guy I've known for twenty years and you've known for two days." He pulled on his slacks and stood up to fasten them. Then he turned to face her while he finished buttoning his shirt.

"That's exactly the point." She raised herself up on one elbow and pulled the sheet over her breasts. "You're too close to the situation. I have a perspective on it that you can't be expected to have. Why can't you make use of my training instead of invalidating it?"

"Why can't you stop being Dr. Newberry for a while?"

"Because it doesn't work that way, Garth. I can't just turn off my brain and become some sort of Stepford Wife while you're around."

"That's ridiculous." He looked around for his shoes. "I've never asked you to be some robot."

"But you've never asked me to help you in an area where I might be of some help, either. That amounts to the same thing."

"And just how would you help?" He picked up his shoes and socks.

"I talked to Boz and I figured out some things. You know why Boz is making a mess of running this place? Because he's given up trying to compete with you. It's easier to be the old, predictable Boz than to risk really putting out some effort and coming up short in comparison to you."

"That's the most farfetched—"

"Test it!" she challenged him. "Talk to him about some of the failures in your life, level the playing field a little, and see if his performance doesn't improve."

Garth sat on a chair and put on his shoes. "You want me to go sniveling to Boz about my failures in life? You think that would help him? And me?"

"Yes."

"Well, you're wrong. It would make him lose all respect for me, that's what it would do." He tied his second shoe and stood up.

"Garth, you are being so bullheaded!"

"Damn right. Being bullheaded has taken me far in this life." He whipped his tie around his neck and knotted it loosely under his unbuttoned collar.

She sat up, still keeping the sheet around her. She fought the inevitable conclusions that assailed her. Garth was intent on keeping up a facade of perfection and self-control. That was why he'd had to blame self-help books for the failure of his marriage. She couldn't afford to fall in love with a man who couldn't admit his mistakes.

Tears filled her eyes. "I shouldn't have come back here. I should have known it wouldn't work between us."

"I think it would work fine if you could keep all that analysis to yourself."

"Yes, that would suit you, wouldn't it?" Misery clogged her throat. "Then you'd never have to examine your feelings, or chance being wrong about something and having to say so. I think Boz has you pegged exactly right, Mr. Perfect. If you ever get tired of that role, let me know. Until then, I think it's best if we don't see each other."

He paused, and his expression closed down. "If that's the way you want it."

"It is."

"I only hope you won't be foolish enough to fly back to Nebraska with that sicko after you."

"Well, I'm pretty foolish, but not that foolish." Her voice shook and she couldn't keep it steady. "I'll stay, assuming your offer of a free room stands."

"It does." Was that a flicker of relief in his eyes? It was gone before she could be sure. "The services of the resort are at your disposal."

"Thank you." She wanted him to leave, so she could cry in peace. He seemed to know it. He turned on his heel and left the suite. She waited until she heard the door close behind him before she flung herself down, muffled her mouth against a pillow and sobbed.

TWO DAYS LATER Garth crouched across the net from Boz and waited for the first serve. "You're sure you're up to this?" he called across the court.

"Once the doc said there was a mix-up in the X rays, I started feeling better already. The question is, are *you* ready? I understand you've been leading a pretty soft life in Boston."

"Give it your best shot," Garth said, swishing through a phantom forehand and backhand. God, he could hardly wait to clobber something. The past two days had been hell, and time spent in the weight room hadn't even begun to take the edge off his frustration.

The serve plowed across the net and Garth smashed it back at Boz. Boz looked startled, but he quickly matched Garth's ferocity and they settled into a vicious exchange that left them both panting and lost Boz his serve.

"I guess you still have the killer instinct," Boz said, mopping the sweat away with the sleeve of his shirt. "Shoulda known."

Something clicked in Garth's mind as he tossed the ball and whacked it into the opposite court, acing Boz. There was something about the way Boz had said, "Shoulda known," as if he'd already accepted defeat, that made Garth think of what Kate had said. Garth pushed the thought away and caught the ball Boz hurled back over the net.

"Nice serve," Boz said.

"Thanks."

"You always did play every game like it was Wimbledon or something."

Garth laughed, but the sound seemed hollow in his ears. "Isn't it?" *Mr. Perfect playing tennis. Stop that, Fredericks! The woman doesn't know what she's talking about.* He served the ball again, but this time Boz returned it and Garth concentrated on scoring the point. After two close calls, he managed it.

He won the set easily, six-two. "Thanks, Boz," he said, throwing an arm over his friend's shoulders as they left the court. "I needed that."

"She hasn't caved in and called you, huh?"

"No." He'd told Boz only that he and Kate had fought, but not why. Neither had he confessed to Boz that the past three nights had been agony as he'd struggled to keep away from her door. The days hadn't been much better. She'd bought herself a sleek little white bathing suit cut high on her thigh and low in the back. He'd seen her on the beach in it twice, in that crazy blond wig. One time she'd pulled a white cover-up over the suit, but the other time she hadn't. If she was trying to torture him, she was doing an excellent job.

Nothing was going well for him. Boz hadn't taken any of the hints he'd thrown out about how to improve the operation of the Pelican. He just smiled and nodded when Garth said something, or changed the subject completely. Garth had suggested hiring a different landscaper, but the same truck as before had pulled up this morning. He'd pointed out that the resort needed a great deal of supervision, yet Boz still took time off whenever he felt like it. Service was as sloppy as ever, despite Garth's observation that all the staff needed reeducating in the art of taking care of people.

Still, the grueling tennis game had helped Garth's mood, even if it hadn't solved any of his problems.

"How about a cool one?" Boz suggested.

"No, I probably—" Garth stopped speaking as he glanced through the plate-glass window in the lobby and saw Kate splashing around at the water's edge. The sight of her in the white suit, with her long slender legs and generous curves, made his gut wrench with longing.

Boz's gaze followed the direction of Garth's. "Sure you wouldn't like a beer?"

"Yeah, come to think of it, I'd love one," Garth said, and turned away from the sight of a blond Kate romping in the waves.

"She'll come around," Boz said as they settled into the dimly lit lounge and ordered their beer. "I'm sure you're playing it right, letting her stew."

"She doesn't exactly look as if she's stewing, Boz. She looks like she's having a damn good time without me."

"She's fakin' it," Boz said, and took a long swallow of the beer the waitress placed in front of him.

"Maybe." Garth tipped the glass and allowed the cool liquid to slide down his throat. It slaked his thirst, but not that other need, the one that gnawed at him whenever he thought about Kate, or worse, saw her, like now. The trouble was, the need wasn't purely physical. If it had been he would have hit the bars around town and found someone to charm. Although he wasn't a stranger to doing that, he couldn't do it now. The prospect seemed— hell, it seemed unfaithful. But unfaithful to what? To whom? That woman cavorting in the surf had no claim on him. Or so he tried to tell himself.

"I tell you, Gartho, you're a barrel of laughs these days."

"Huh?"

"Just love sitting in a bar with you, buddy, watching you drink and stare into space. She got you buffaloed or something?"

"Of course not." He raised his glass. "I—" Garth stopped in midsentence as it occurred to him that he was doing exactly what Kate had accused him of—pretending that nothing bothered him, that he was some sort of

superman. And he was pretending that to his best friend.
He put down the glass. "She's driving me crazy," he said,
not looking at Boz.

"You? Ironman Fredericks?"

"Yeah, me." He glanced at Boz. "I want her, Boz, and
I don't think she wants me. At least not the way I am."

"Then she's a stupid female. Any woman would be
glad to have a stud like you. Even if Judith took half your
money, you still have enough left to make some little
sweetie pret-ty happy."

"Kate's not interested in my money-making abilities."

"All right. There are other attractions. You're a de-
cent-looking guy, and usually good company, the past
two days excepted."

Garth shrugged. Now that he'd opened this door of
self-revelation he wondered if he had the courage to step
through it.

"So what's the problem? Is she into kinky sex or
something? I mean, I haven't read her book, but—"

Garth gave him a wry smile. "She'd have a fit if she
heard you say that. No, she's very normal, and very
wonderful." He hesitated, then took a deep breath and
let it out. "Unfortunately, she thinks I have an unfixable
flaw."

Boz was silent for a moment. "Like what?"

"I won't admit my mistakes."

"That's hard to do when you don't make any."

Garth pushed his glass away and stood. "I don't need
cracks like that, Boz."

"Cracks? What cracks? I mean it."

"Come off it." Kate's words rang in his head. *He says you don't make mistakes.*

"I'm being straight with you, Gartho. I'm the screwup of this team, not you." He ticked items off on his fingers. "I never finished college. I don't have any real career. I'm divorced. I—"

"I'm divorced."

"Yeah, but in my case, I was part of the problem. I wasn't earning much of a living because I like to party too much. In your case, Judith got hooked on those books, which didn't have much to do with you."

Garth returned to his seat. "Or so I've tried to tell myself."

"What do you mean?"

"Well . . ." Garth sighed. "I've been thinking about Judith. Whenever I wasn't thinking about Kate, that is. Anyway, I finally admitted to myself that I'd stopped loving her long before this business came up with the self-help books."

"No kidding? Do you think she knew?"

Garth nodded. "Sure, on some level. The books were probably a way to get my attention. But her method backfired. I used those books as an excuse to get a divorce."

Boz stared into his empty beer glass for a long time. "Kinda makes me feel sorry for Judith. She couldn't win."

"That's right. Pretty lousy way to treat someone, wouldn't you say?"

Boz roused himself. "Hey, it's not like you knew what you were doing."

"Maybe if I'd read a few of those books I'd have figured out what I was doing, though."

"So then what? You can't be blamed for not loving her anymore."

"No, but I can be blamed for making her take the rap, when the divorce was really my fault." As Garth talked, he was surprised that he felt better—not worse—for having said this. Maybe his conscience had known it all the time, but his brain hadn't let the information through.

"So what are you going to do?"

"Apologize to Judith, for one thing."

Boz stared at him. "You're not going back to her, are you?"

"No. I really don't love her anymore, which sure isn't her fault. Sometimes these things happen. People's needs change."

Boz nodded.

Garth decided to try something else. He wondered how long it had been since he'd asked anyone's advice about anything. He glanced at Boz. "What do you think I should do about Kate?"

Boz looked startled, but he quickly covered his expression with one of thoughtful concentration. Finally he answered, his voice measured and steady. The way, Garth thought, he himself had probably spoken to Boz hundreds of times in the past.

"I think," Boz said, "that you should read her book."

13

EDDIE GUMP was not a happy man. Torrential rains slapped against the window of his motel room while he sat and stared at afternoon cartoons on TV. The bitch wasn't in Northbluff. He'd found her address in the phone book, had watched her place until his butt got numb. He'd stayed low, in case she'd told somebody to keep an eye out for him, but he'd still managed to keep pretty close track of her house. She wasn't there.

Finally he'd called the college and pretended to be a student looking for her. Some superior broad had told him Dr. Newberry would be back next week. Next week! Dammit, he should have watched that airport rest room until she came out and headed toward the gate. He should have made sure she got on the plane. Now he'd lost her.

Eddie rested his head in his hands and tried to think. His money was almost gone, but he still had his gas credit card, which had come in handy when he'd blown a tire in Colorado. Good thing he liked fast food. He could afford a few more hamburgers and tacos, maybe get through another three or four days, if he was careful.

He could head back to Houston and be there before the money ran out. He could do that, except that then the bitch would keep getting away with it, keep corrupting women like his Janey. He owed it to guys like himself to stop this Dr. Kate and stop her cold.

He knew she'd be in L.A. for that talk show in a few days, but he didn't have enough cash to last until then. He had an idea. It wasn't much to go on, but he wondered if she'd somehow doubled back to the resort and figured on staying there until the talk show. He'd probably made a bad move, putting the note in the basket of rolls. He'd wanted to see her face looking scared one more time, in front of all those people, but he'd kept her away from Nebraska.

Maybe she *was* back in San Diego, lolling in the sunshine, while he sat in the middle of this miserable rain. The thought made him clench his fists and grind his teeth. If she'd done that to him, made him suffer like this for nothing, he'd get her double. Thinking about the sweetness of that moment when he'd cut her down to size made him smile. Yep, first thing in the morning he'd start south. If nothing else, the weather would be better.

KATE RATIONED HERSELF one phone call a day to stave off loneliness. On that first night after Garth's defection, as she liked to term it, she called Donna. As Kate had expected she would, Donna championed her decision to send this new man packing if he couldn't respect her profession. Donna was less encouraging about Kate's future at Northbluff.

The sensational events at the Pelican had made the Nebraska papers, and Donna said there were rumblings among the older faculty members that Kate lacked the right "tone" for Northbluff College. Donna assured Kate that her three friends were doing what they could, but they didn't have much pull, considering that all of them were considered rebels and therefore were in uneasy circumstances themselves.

The second night Kate called her sister, but the conversation was interrupted numerous times by the needs of her sister's children. Kate finally gave up the effort and went to bed early, which only resulted in a longer, more restless night. At one point she thought it was a blessing that she had no idea where Garth's room was. At three in the morning, her defenses down and her needs at an all-time high, she would have gone there and easily relinquished her pride in exchange for the excitement she'd found in his arms.

The third night she called her agent.

"So you're lonely," Glenda said without much evidence of sympathy. "Pretty soon you're going to be so rich you can buy a nice man. Fan letters are pouring in, and next week I predict you'll make the *Times* list."

"Send me the letters," Kate said. "Put them in an envelope to Leticia Throckmorton. I could use a lift right now."

"Sweetheart, have you read your own book? Don't let this Garth fellow get to you this way. Aren't you the one who tells women not to let men pull their chain all the time?"

"Don't remind me." Kate knew she sounded peevish. "I'm sorry," she added with a sigh. "I'll be okay once I get away from here and can settle down to a normal existence somehow. Of course, that's assuming I can. My friend Donna says Northbluff's in an uproar over all my unfavorable publicity."

"Unfavorable? Honey, that's the stuff that stars are made of!"

"I have the soul of a scholar, Glenda, not a star."

"Nonsense. Wait'll that first royalty check arrives. Incidentally, speaking of publicity, any sign of your crazy guy?"

"No. That's something, at least. I guess the plan worked. He's probably crawled back under his rock."

"I wish they'd caught him."

"Me, too, but at least he's been thrown off the track. Listen, send me those letters, okay?"

"I will, but in the meantime I suggest you reread Chapter Nine in your book. You know the one I mean?"

"Yes, Glenda, I know. I wrote it."

"Then show me you can practice what you preach. Good night, now."

"Good night." Kate hung up the phone and wandered around the suite. Remembered snippets of the chapter Glenda was talking about taunted her as she fought down her longing for Garth. The chapter was titled "Princes and Frogs." She couldn't deny that Garth sometimes acted like a frog; the trouble was, no matter how many times she reminded herself of that, she couldn't erase the fact that he made love like a prince.

THE NEXT DAY Kate arose with new resolve to enjoy the remaining time at the Pelican whether or not Garth was acting like a frog. She spent the morning strolling the streets of La Jolla, carefully dressed in her wig. She splurged on a half-priced turquoise jumpsuit in one of the boutiques. As she noticed the cars parked along the curb beside the shop—a Mercedes here, a Corvette there, and a Rolls-Royce in between—she thought about Glenda's comment that she would soon be rich.

Maybe she, too, would be able to afford a prestige car. Maybe she'd be able to wander into any of the trendy stores along Prospect Street and buy whatever struck her fancy, on sale or not. Unfortunately the idea didn't appeal to her. She longed for a classroom of eager freshmen, a quiet night going over her lecture notes, an entire day spent browsing the musty shelves of the Northbluff College library. Glenda lived a fast-paced life in New York. She couldn't be expected to understand.

Strangely enough, Kate knew Garth would understand. But that didn't stack up against the things Garth didn't understand, and besides, she'd promised herself to forget him for one day. Determined to enjoy herself, she bought a coffee ice-cream cone from Baskin Robbins and took the coast walk back to the Pelican. The path skirted the edge of the cliffs overlooking La Jolla Cove and eventually dipped down into a residential area just behind the Pelican.

From the top of the cliffs Kate had a sweeping view of the shoreline. Pelicans and gulls swooped toward her and settled below on shallow outcroppings. The salty tang of the breeze made her take a deep breath. The sun on her face felt good. Maybe she could enjoy life despite Garth's behavior, after all.

She maintained her confident stride and determined cheerfulness until she reached the tennis courts and saw

Garth there, his body arching into a serve. She felt as if it were her heart Garth was smashing over the net onto the clay court opposite him.

She watched longer than she should have. He hadn't seen her, but she'd absorbed enough of his magnetism to turn her resolve into aching need. Cursing herself for falling in love with an unacceptable man, exactly the thing she'd disparaged in her book, she fled into the lobby and up to her room. There she changed into her suit and raced back down to the beach, where she splashed through the waves until the urge to throw herself into Garth's arms had subsided to a dull, persistent throb of frustration.

She ate dinner in her room that night and sat through a movie about aliens that numbed her senses. Finally she crawled into bed and switched out the lights. As the minutes ticked away on the bedside clock, she lay and listened to the soft swish of waves outside her sliding glass door. Eventually the rhythm worked on her, and she slept.

She awoke in the darkness, aware of something. Then the sound came again, a soft tapping at the door to her suite. She glanced at the clock: two-thirty in the morning. Her heart began to pound as she swung her feet to the floor. Okay, so it might be Garth. Who else would tap on her door at this hour?

But if he hadn't reformed his opinions, she wouldn't let him in. She'd open the door a crack and ask what his intentions were. If he couldn't answer to her satisfaction, she'd close and lock the door. She wouldn't let him in, let his sensual appeal override her better judgment.

Absolutely not, she vowed as she padded toward the door without bothering to turn on any lights and stood on tiptoe to peer through the peephole.

When she saw it was Garth, standing there in his nylon running shorts and T-shirt and looking like the answer to her prayers, she flung open the door.

He stepped inside, closed the door with a firm click and took her in his arms. "I need you so damn much," he muttered into her hair as he kissed her earlobe, her chin, and at last her lips. With a sigh she gave up every noble thought she'd had on the way to the door. Nothing else mattered but this—the caress of his hands in the velvet darkness, the sound of his breathing, the taste of his mouth.

He guided her into the bedroom and she went willingly. The thin bits of material covering them fell away and they slid into bed together with as much joy as dolphins arcing gracefully through the waves.

Kate laughed with pleasure as Garth stroked the length of her body and made her skin sing. She mimicked his movement and traced the sinewed strength of him from shoulder to thigh. He was so warm, so ready to love her. She touched him with greedy hands and felt him shudder, heard his sigh of surrender.

His mouth sought hers again, his tongue probing, suggesting, teasing and drawing back. She grew moist, impatient. Her fingers curled around his shaft and in answer he groaned and moved above her. No fumbling in the bedside drawer this time, no apparent worry about making her pregnant.

"Garth?"

"It doesn't matter. We're getting married. We're having children."

"How do you know I want children?"

He hesitated. "Don't you?"

"Yes, but—"

His kiss silenced her as he thrust forward, giving her no time to think as the sensation of loving him cascaded through her. She held on to him, rising to meet each thrust, desperately wanting the union, the completion that he offered. With a cry she surged over the edge of control and carried him with her. Gasping, he braced himself on his arms although she tried to hold him close, to cradle him against her body.

"No," he said, his jaw clenched.

Still quivering herself, she gazed up at him in the dim gray light as strong spasms rocked his body, making the cords stand out in his neck. His eyes closed and his lips parted, but he stayed braced firmly above her.

At last his breathing steadied and he opened his eyes. "See?" he murmured, smiling at her. "I'm awake."

She tried to pull him to her. "Garth, you—"

"I'll come closer," he said, lowering himself onto his elbows, "but I can't get too settled in. You're right about that narcoleptic state, and I can't afford it. I have a few things to say."

"I think you said them."

"Not everything, not nearly everything. I had a whole speech ready, but when I saw you standing in the doorway in that flimsy white gown, I lost whatever self-control I had left after all this time without you."

"Me, too." She held his face in her hands. "I wasn't going to open the door unless you said all the right things, either."

"But you did open the door."

"Yes."

"I hope for the reason I think."

She looked deep into his eyes, so soft in the darkness. "I love you, Garth. Is that the reason you wanted?"

"Yes." He kissed her tenderly, his lips paying reverent homage to hers. "Yes," he murmured again, "because I love you, and if you don't love me back, we'd have a very rocky marriage."

"We may have one anyway," she said, speaking against the feather pressure of his mouth.

He lifted his head. "You think so?"

"We don't exactly agree on everything, Garth."

He rested his cheek on his fist and smiled. "'A couple has an excellent chance of success if they have a shared value system. More than sexual compatibility or common interests, a shared value system cements a long-lasting union.'"

Kate's eyes widened. "I wrote that."

"I know."

"You read my book!"

"Finished it about a half hour ago."

"Oh, Garth." Her eyes filled with tears of happiness. "I think that means as much as your telling me you loved me."

"That's because reading the book means I love you." He caressed her cheek. "And by not reading it before, I made a big mistake, one that's cost us a lot of unnecessary heartbreak. I'm sorry, Kate."

Kate's heart thudded. "Do you know what you just said?"

"Absolutely. I made a mistake, Kate. But I have to confess, you're not the first woman who heard me say that. Earlier tonight I called Judith."

Fear chilled her.

"Hey, don't look like that. I meant it when I said I don't love Judith anymore. But I really mangled the whole divorce business. Instead of admitting I didn't love her, I kept up our charade of a marriage, always making sure we didn't have kids to worry about, and waited for her to stir up trouble. She did, using self-help books, and I had my scapegoat. I just called her tonight to confess my sins."

Kate tried to talk around the lump in her throat. "What did she say?"

"Well, she cried, which made me feel like even more of a heel, but she thinks now she'll be able to put her own life together again and really let go of her feelings for me, which include rage, I'm sure."

She drew his head down for a lingering kiss. "My prince."

He chuckled. "Watch out, I may still have some frog tendencies lurking around." He nuzzled her neck. "Ribbet, ribbet."

"I'll take my chances."

"Pretty risky." He kissed his way down to the tip of one breast. "Dr. Kate would advise more caution than you're displaying, young lady."

"When Dr. Kate wrote her book, I don't think she imagined someone like you." Desire funneled downward, setting her afire once more. "Oh, Garth, I want you again."

"Hmm. I read somewhere that long, exquisite foreplay is every woman's dream." He dipped his tongue into her navel. "Don't rush me."

THE NEXT MORNING Garth moved his belongings into the suite. "The ultimate test of a relationship," he pronounced as he positioned his shaving gear on the counter next to her cosmetics. "Sharing a bathroom. As I seem to recall, you take a long time to put on makeup."

"Wrong, Mr. Fredericks." She leaned against the bathroom doorframe, clad only in the white terry-cloth robe provided by the resort. "When I was on the publicity tour I took a long time to put on makeup. I was instructed to look like that, and the publisher was paying for everything, so I cooperated. Leticia Throckmorton uses scarcely any makeup."

"I see." He turned from the counter to gaze at her. "That's because she doesn't need it. God, you're beautiful."

She blushed, embarrassed. "Thank you."

He stepped forward and touched her pink cheeks. "And to think I had an image of you as some polished sophisticate."

"It was all a veneer, Garth. You should see me at home in Nebraska grading term papers, with my hair tied back, wearing baggy sweats."

"Sounds wonderful to me."

"I think you'd like it there. You—" She stopped. Still basking in the glow of their shared love, she hated to get too specific and risk spoiling the mood, but it had occurred to her that her life and Garth's might not be so easy to mesh. "Have you, um, thought about our future?"

"Constantly. That is, when I wasn't completely engaged in making love to you. I think in Chapter Five you talk about how irritated women get when they suspect a man isn't concentrating totally on the lovemaking, so let me assure you that I—"

Kate laughed. "Give it a rest, Garth. I'm convinced you read the whole book. I think you memorized parts of it."

"It was a good book."

"Thank you."

His expression was earnest. "I knew after reading it that I wanted to marry you. We think alike."

"That's great, but what about things like where we're going to live?"

"I gather you really like Nebraska."

"Yes, especially Northbluff. I like the change of seasons, the ivy-covered buildings, the—"

"Then we'll live there. Next question?"

She wasn't used to such quick decision making. "Just like that?"

"Sure. I operate with a computer and a telephone, mostly. A friend of mine has been trying to woo my secretary away for years, so she'll have a job if I leave Boston."

"Northbluff isn't very high-powered. We have one movie house and three decent restaurants, if you don't count the truck stop."

Garth drew her close. "I was serious last night when I quoted that part in your book about value systems. I've lived a fairly high-profile life, but I don't need it, don't even want it anymore. Northbluff sounds wonderful to me. We'll have a simple life."

"Oh, I hope so." She leaned her head into the hollow of his shoulder.

"Unless you keep writing these blockbuster books of yours."

Kate groaned. "Never again. I hope I can manage to live down this one."

"You will. People forget faster than you think, and in the meantime I'll stand guard at the gate."

"I love you so much."

"Enough to let me have first dibs on the bathroom? I'm supposed to meet Boz in about fifteen minutes."

"Oh?" She raised her head and looked at him.

"I thought about canceling out, but the more I think about it, the more I think I'd better go. I have some unfinished business with my old buddy, too."

Kate held her breath. This charged topic had been their undoing three days earlier.

"Yesterday I admitted to Boz what a mess I'd made with Judith. Today I'd better get this resort management business out in the open. I think you were on to something with what you said—I may have done Boz more harm than good over the years."

She let out her breath. "I'm not sure I'd go that far. You've given him undemanding friendship."

"Yeah. And maybe I needed him to be inept, so I could look better in comparison."

"Wow." Kate smiled at him. "Pretty soon you'll be ready to hang out your shingle. When you grab hold of an idea, you really grab hold."

"And you're the same way."

She nodded. "That's why I wrote the book."

"And why we're going to have one hell of a life. Neither of us likes doing things halfway. Which is why you need to leave this bathroom." He gave her a little shove out the door.

"Hey!" She pretended to be indignant.

"We don't have time for anything more than a halfway job of making love, and if you stick around, I'll be tempted to try even that. So go away, you sexy woman, and let me shave in peace."

Smiling to herself, Kate left the bathroom to make a list of all the people she wanted to call with her good news. Garth and a life as a college professor in North-bluff. It looked as if she *could* have it all!

14

GARTH BARELY MADE IT out the door in time. At the last minute he had to have one last kiss, and Kate's robe accidentally fell open. She was the one who finally reminded him that Boz was waiting and tied her robe firmly in place.

"I'll be back as soon as I can. It's hard to say how long this discussion will take," he said at the door.

"I know. Don't rush it."

"But I want—"

She laid her finger across his lips. "I know. I'll be here. I have some calls to make, anyway."

"Tell them I'm crazy about you and we'll be married as soon as you set the date."

She laughed. "How do you know these calls are about us?"

"By the look in your eyes." He dropped a quick kiss on her cheek. "I'll be back soon."

Kate closed and locked the door behind him before crossing to the telephone. First she'd call Donna, who had a free hour right now and would be in her office.

The sound of Donna's throaty voice made Kate hug herself with happiness. Donna and Garth would get along; she just knew it.

"Anybody with you right now?" she asked.

"Kate! Nope, I'm all alone. What's up?"

"My frog turned into a prince."

"No kidding? Details, kiddo. Give me details."

Kate gave her details. "I know I'm speaking in superlatives, Donna, but he's so great. And he wants to live in Northbluff with me! Can you believe it?"

There was a hesitation on the other line. "I hope that's possible."

"Oh, Donna, don't tell me they're throwing me out." The shine rubbed right off of Kate's day.

"Some of the faculty members believe you'll keep writing books like this. They're all upset about the guy on your trail and the incident with the manager of your hotel. They think Northbluff College will turn into a circus if you're around. No way do they want to get involved in tabloid craziness, as they call it."

"Listen, Donna. I'm not writing any more books. Garth and I want a quiet life. We're agreed on that. The committee has to understand that this will die down soon. You know how it is. Today everybody knows who you are, and tomorrow your face is lining bird cages."

"But, Kate, you could sell another book in a minute and make tons of money. If I were you I'd forget those stodgies at Northbluff and go for it."

"Take it from me, being a celebrity is no bed of roses. No, I want off this merry-go-round. Do you think if I wrote a letter personally promising the committee that I had no plans to publish another book they'd settle down?"

Donna hesitated. "Maybe. I guess it's worth a shot."

"Sounds like my only shot. I'll borrow a typewriter and do it today."

"The sooner the better. The woman you got to take your classes is incredibly boring—the students don't much like her—but she's already in tight with the rest of the faculty. Our bunch excluded, of course."

"I'm going to save that job," Kate vowed. "Say hello to Jennie and Ann for me, and thanks for what you three have done."

"You bet. Good luck."

Kate hung up and dialed room service to order a typewriter. After some discussion, during which Kate learned there was only one in the building because everyone used computers, she was promised that a bellman would arrive soon with the machine.

She decided to shower and dress immediately so she could take the letter to the post office herself once she'd typed it. She might even send it in the overnight mail. By the time a rap sounded on the door she was dressed in her new turquoise jumpsuit, although her hair was still damp.

Mentally composing her plea to the Northbluff faculty committee, she hurried to the door and opened it.

A man stood there, his sandy hair in disarray. "Hello, Dr. Kate," he said.

AS HE WALKED through the lobby on his way to Boz's office, Garth noticed that a different company's landscaping truck was parked in the circular driveway. He wondered if Boz had decided to take one of his suggestions, after all.

He tapped on the partially open office door and walked in. The sight that greeted him made his mouth drop open.

"What's the matter?" Boz asked with a grin. "Never seen a guy in a suit and tie before?"

"I wasn't sure you owned one."

Boz loosened the knot of the tie a notch. "Not the most comfortable getup in the world, but I found out a funny thing when I wore it this morning. The staff treated me differently."

Garth nodded, still dumbfounded by the change in Boz. Even the office looked neater, the desk more orderly.

"I'm trying out some new landscape company," Boz said. "Called around and got some bids, and these guys weren't the cheapest, but they work on some of the other top places in town, so we'll see."

"Good. Very good." Garth lowered himself into a chair opposite Boz's desk.

"I've also called a staff meeting for this afternoon. Want to sit in on it? I thought we'd go over procedures and see how we can improve the service around here."

"I—I doubt you'll need me, Boz." For the first time since he'd arrived in La Jolla, Garth believed that. "You know, I came here this morning to talk about just this sort of thing."

"Yeah." Boz leaned back in his chair. "You've been pretty ticked off about how I've run the place, right?"

"Maybe 'ticked off' isn't the right word, but—"

"Aw, hell, Gartho. Ticked off is exactly the word. I've known it, but I couldn't seem to take myself in hand, somehow."

"So what do you call all this?" Garth gestured around the clean office. "Looks like you've been pretty busy since we talked yesterday."

"Yeah. Guess it's about time, huh?"

Garth rubbed his chin and stared at Boz. "Why now?"

Boz grinned. "Damned if I know."

"I think you do," Garth said softly. "I think it's because yesterday for the first time in twenty years I admitted to you that I was human. That I wasn't 'Mr. Perfect.'"

Boz looked startled. "Kate must have told you I said that. Listen, I didn't mean it in a bad way. I—"

"No, you listen." Garth leaned forward. "All these years I've thought of myself as such a good friend, always helping you."

"You have been!"

"No. Because I made sure it was a one-way street. I never admitted any weakness, so you couldn't help me back. That made me the big man, the hero. I don't blame you for resenting the hell out of me, Boz."

"Garth, I don't resent you. You've been my best friend. You've—"

"I've never let you see me sweat. Not until yesterday. Think about it. Think about the fact that I finally told you I'd messed up with Judith. And then you were able to give me some advice. It may have been the best advice anyone's ever given me, Boz. I read Kate's book."

"You did?" Boz's face lit up. "Have you told her?"

Garth chuckled. "A few times. We're getting married, Boz."

"Hot damn." Boz leapt from his chair and rounded the desk. "Way to go, Gartho," he said, giving him a high five. "This calls for a drink."

"Of coffee. It's still morning, buddy."

"Of course we'll have coffee," Boz said, his tone injured. "I have a staff meeting to conduct this afternoon."

"And I have . . . well, I have things to do, too."

"I won't ask," Boz said.

"Good."

"But why don't we have Kate join us? Hell, we can toast with coffee as well as we can with champagne."

"Good idea." Garth reached for the desk phone. "I'll call the room."

"I notice you said *the* room. Does that mean you two are sharing again?"

"Everything," Garth said as he listened to the phone ring. "Maybe she's in the shower. She promised not to leave without telling me." He replaced the receiver. "Tell you what. Fill me in on what you're going to say at the staff meeting. I'll try her again in a few minutes."

KATE HURLED her weight against the door, but the man moved faster. The door was wrenched from her grasp as he forced his way inside and tackled her, wrestling her to the floor. She tried to scream. Her breath was gone, knocked away by the force of her fall and his weight on her. He kicked at the door and it closed behind him.

"Well, now, Dr. Kate." His eyes were ice blue and filled with demonic anger. "We meet at last."

"You'll be caught," she whispered. The smell of him revolted her. She struggled under his heavy weight. He was pushing the breath out of her. She got one hand free and grabbed at his face.

He caught her wrist before she could gouge him with her nails. Then he fumbled for her other wrist and held her hands above her head. "I won't be caught."

"Yes," she gasped. "Yes, you will."

"No." He held her wrists with one hand and squeezed her jaw with the other. "Because after I'm through with you, you won't want them to catch me."

She stared at him in disbelief.

"You've never had it like you're gonna have it now, Dr. Kate." His eyes glittered and saliva thickened his speech. The mole beside his nose quivered as he talked. "You're gonna love it. You'll beg me for more. You'll help me get away, so we can go somewhere more private. You don't know what a real man is like, do you? I'm gonna show you, and show you good. Show you that the crap you're writing ain't worth nothing."

Fear twisted in her gut. She tried to think. Maybe she could stall. Garth would be coming back. But she'd told him to take his time. *Say something,* she told herself. *Distract him.* "What's your name?"

"Now that's more like it. You'll be moaning my name pretty soon. The name's Eddie. Eddie's the man who's gonna get you right with the world, Dr. Kate. All them college degrees. You think you know how it's done, but you don't know nothing."

She had to get him off her if she expected to make a break for it. Her throat was closed but she had to talk to him. "Listen . . . Eddie. Wouldn't we be more comfortable on—" she swallowed bile rising in her throat "—the bed?" she choked out.

"I like the floor."

"But I—"

"Shut up!" He squeezed her cheeks. "I don't give a damn what you like! Get that?" His hooked nose made him look like some crazed bird of prey. "I'm not some wimp who runs around asking you what you want and when you want it. You'll get no satisfaction from a man like that. You know why? Because you run him. Women get satisfaction from a man who shows them who's boss. And I'm gonna show you, baby." Holding her jaw, he swooped down, his mouth open and dripping.

Nausea rose in her as his wet mouth slobbered against hers. He held her teeth apart so she couldn't bite the tongue he shoved into her mouth. She gagged.

He wrenched her arms higher over her head to punish her for gagging. Her shoulders ached. She twisted beneath him. Somehow she'd get her knee up. She'd do it. Using all her strength, she wrenched her knee up in the direction of his crotch. And missed.

He let loose of her jaw and grabbed her leg, twisting it painfully to one side. He glared down at her. "Since you won't be still and take your medicine, guess we'll have to go find that private place now."

She was panting and sweat streamed from her. "You can't take me out of here. There are people everywhere. They'll—"

"They'll think you're a little drunk," he said, and pulled a cloth from his back pocket.

"No!" She saw the cloth descend, smelled the chloroform, and the room began to spin.

AFTER BOZ FINISHED outlining his approach to the staff meeting, Garth nodded in approval. "Should be very effective."

"Sure you don't want to sit in?"

"Yep, I'm sure. Other things to do. Which reminds me, I'll try Kate one more time." He picked up the phone and dialed. Still no answer. He frowned as the phone continued to ring. He'd left her less than a half hour ago. Nothing could happen in a half hour, unless . . . He slammed down the phone. "We're going up there."

"You don't look so hot."

"Paranoia, I guess," he said over his shoulder as he headed out of Boz's office. "I just don't like the idea that I couldn't reach her."

"Probably in the shower."

"Yeah," Garth said, not believing it. "Let's take the stairs." He jerked open the fire door and started up.

"This is why I don't wear suits and ties," Boz complained, puffing a little to keep up.

"Sorry." Garth slowed his pace a bit. "I'm being silly about this. Kate'll get a good laugh out of it."

"So will I, once I catch my breath."

"Love can make you crazy, you know?" Garth opened the fire door onto the second floor and held it for Boz. "You start imagining dangers where none exist. You—"

"The suite door's open."

Garth whirled. Kate wouldn't leave it like that. Calling her name, he charged forward with Boz right behind. He skidded to a stop inside the sitting room. "Kate!" He knew immediately she wasn't there. Dashing through the bedroom he saw evidence of her shower—a discarded towel, a bathroom light still on.

He flung open the sliding door to the balcony and shaded his eyes against the sun as he leaned over the railing. "Kate!" he called again.

"Garth, I found her purse," Boz said, hurrying into the bedroom. "She wouldn't leave without her purse."

KATE TRIED to resist the effects of the chloroform as she drifted in and out of consciousness. She was in danger. She had to fight. Had to scream. She opened her mouth, but nothing came out. There was a ringing sound. She tried to remember what that meant. Vaguely she realized she was being carried down the fire stairs. Garth. Where was Garth?

The coolness of the stairway revived her a little. She tried to free herself from the man's grip. "Let me go!" she shouted, but her shout came out as a whisper.

He dragged her, stumbling and trying to resist him, across the service parking lot toward a truck. "Don't fight me," he warned her, "or it will go harder for you later on."

"Garth will kill you," she croaked. Her throat was raw and she was dizzy. So dizzy. She wanted to rest, but she couldn't rest. She had to get away.

He yanked open the truck's door and pushed her inside. She kicked at him but didn't connect.

"That'll cost you," he said, breathing hard as he slammed the truck door. "You'll be giving me some special treats for that, Dr. Kate. Treats I'll bet you don't usually give to guys. But you'll give them to me."

Kate tried to focus on the scene around her. Was anybody there to help? If only she could yell . . . but her vocal cords wouldn't work right. She reached for the horn on the steering column and batted at it. A bleep of sound came out.

"Now you're really in trouble," he said, starting to climb behind the wheel.

She groaned in despair as he started to close the door of the cab. *Really in trouble.*

"I'll get you good," he said, slamming the door. "I'll—"

The door flew open. Hands grabbed at Eddie, yanked him out. Kate leaned over, trying to focus on what had happened. Garth! Garth had the man on the ground. And farther away came Boz, running. She was saved.

GARTH PLANTED his knees in the guy's back and pinned him to the pavement facedown. The guy was screaming, but Garth didn't care. "See about Kate!" he shouted at Boz.

He grabbed a handful of hair and pulled the guy's head back.

"Breakin' my neck!" choked the guy.

"So what? What's your goddamn name, bastard?" Garth pulled harder.

"Eddie! Eddie Gump! Stop it!"

Boz clamped a hand on his wrist. "Easy, Gartho. You're killing the guy. I yelled at somebody in the kitchen to call the police. Let them handle this slime."

Garth tried to wrench free but Boz held on. "I want to kill him, Boz. Kate—how's Kate?"

"She'll be okay." A siren sounded in the distance and came closer. "Groggy, that's all. She'll be okay."

Garth managed to pull the guy's head back another notch. "What'd you do to her, dirt bag?"

The man started to squeal. "I wouldn'ta hurt her. I wouldn'ta hurt her."

"Liar!" Garth strained the man's windpipe until the squealing stopped. The siren's wail drew near.

"Easy," Boz said, tightening his hold on Garth's wrist. "You'll break his neck. He used a little chloroform, judging from the smell. Kate will be okay."

"She'd better be," Garth said raggedly as a police car screeched to a stop next to them. "Or I'll personally take care of you, you son of a bitch." He gave the man's head another jerk before easing himself away as the police approached.

Once the police had the man handcuffed and had checked Kate's condition, they radioed for paramedics to give her a more thorough examination. Garth sat in the truck and held her until they arrived. She was like a sleepy child, disoriented and cranky. The police found the chloroform-saturated cloth in the guy's hip pocket.

As Garth held Kate and rocked her gently, he thought of what might have happened if he and Boz hadn't come to such a quick agreement about the resort, if the talk they'd had the day before hadn't paved the way for their new understanding. The longer they'd stayed in Boz's office, the greater the chance this creep would have taken

Kate away. Garth shuddered. Whatever it took, he would make certain that she stayed safe from now on.

WITH THE HELP of extra-strength aspirin, Kate's headache was receding. She lay huddled in Garth's arms, swathed in his faithful old sweat suit. She was supposed to be sleeping, but she couldn't sleep, even though the man had been taken away by the police. She'd seen that. He was caught. And Garth had promised her he'd do everything possible to make sure the creep stayed that way.

Garth had never left her side. When they'd returned to the room at last, Kate had showered until her skin started to wrinkle. At last she'd put on his soft sweat suit and crawled into bed with Garth, who held her close. His even breathing and softly pumping heart soothed her, but she couldn't sleep.

She remembered the typewriter again. Had someone delivered it, after all? She lifted her face away from the shelter of Garth's shoulder. "I have something I have to do."

He gazed down at her and kissed her brow. "Yes. You have to relax. I can tell your mind's racing a mile a minute. Your headache won't go away if you don't try to blank everything out."

"My headache's a lot better, and I can't relax until I've written a letter to Northbluff College. Was there a typewriter in the sitting room when we came back?"

"Yeah. I wondered about that."

Kate extricated herself from his arms and sat up. "I have to type that letter." She swung her feet to the floor. "Our future may depend on it."

"Whoa." He reached a hand around her waist and hauled her back. "Tell me what this is all about."

"I talked to my friend Donna and she said the faculty committee may decide not to renew my contract. They don't like all this adverse publicity. I'm sending them a letter promising there will be no more books. Maybe that will help. I wanted to put it in the mail today."

Garth released her and got out of bed himself. "Okay. You dictate and I'll type. Then we'll fax it from the office downstairs. Think it would help if you told them you'll soon be a married woman?"

"Maybe." Kate smiled at him. "You're willing to put that in black and white for the faculty of Northbluff?"

"I'm willing to have it written across the sky in every major city in the world."

Kate gazed at him and the last of the ice that had formed around her heart during the past few hours fell away. She'd be okay now. "Then let's get to work."

In the sitting room she pulled back the drapes with a flourish and opened the sliding door to let in the late-afternoon sun and the sounds of activity on the beach. He was gone. Eddie Gump was sitting in a jail in San Diego, and he couldn't bother her anymore.

The telephone rang and she tensed. The sound still brought back unpleasant memories.

"I'll get it," Garth said.

She decided to let him continue to stand guard. In a little while, when she'd had more time to recover, she'd answer her own phones and her own doorbells, but not quite yet. She listened to Garth's tone of voice as he talked with someone on the other end. She detected nothing wrong.

"Sure. Send it up." He replaced the receiver. "A large packet for Leticia Throckmorton," he said, turning toward her. "Was Leticia expecting something?"

Kate shook her head. Then she remembered. "My agent Glenda promised to send along some fan mail."

"Let me answer the door."

"Gladly. I'm bracing myself for the first visits from the press."

"We'll hold them off as long as we can, but you know you'll have to face them eventually."

"I know. There's still that talk-show appearance on Saturday, for one thing."

Garth's mouth set in a straight line. "I wish you didn't have to do that."

"So do I, but I promised. Backing out now would be unprofessional."

Someone knocked on the door. "Mail for Mrs. Throckmorton," the messenger called.

Garth glanced at her and grinned. "And I thought I was the only male for Mrs. Throckmorton," he said in a low voice.

"You are," she whispered, and blew him a kiss before he went to open the door.

In a few seconds he returned with a padded envelope the size of a bed pillow. "A *few* fan letters? Looks like you get more letters than Santa Claus." He handed her the package.

Kate hefted it in amazement. Then she ripped open the drawstring and a torrent of envelopes spilled out. "My goodness." She sat on the floor and started picking them up. They carried return addresses from all over the country, not just cities where she'd spoken.

"Want a letter opener?"

"We shouldn't bother with this now." She continued sorting through the letters. They came from Baltimore, Springfield, Atlanta, Salem, Colorado Springs and Akron, in white envelopes, pink ones, flowered ones, embossed ones, scented ones and the kind that cost a dollar for a package of fifty. All sorts of women, in all sorts of circumstances, had responded to her book.

"I'll get the letter opener," Garth said.

When he returned with it, Kate slit open an envelope and pulled out the contents. The paper was blue and had lines on it. In one corner was a sprig of violets.

You have changed my life. Because of what you wrote I broke up with my boyfriend, who didn't treat me right, and I've started dating a nice man from work who seems to pass all the tests you put in your book. I am happier than I have ever been. Your book is my bible.

Sincerely,
Tracey Potts

Kate handed the letter to Garth and slit open another.

Your perceptive evaluation of the male-female relationship has enhanced my marriage and given me invaluable advice to pass on to my teenage daughter. After reading your book, I've realized that my husband really is a gem. Our tiny disagreements and breakdowns in communication are not enough to destroy a marriage. Now that I understand that we share the same values, I am much more appreciative.

Very truly yours,
Amanda Emerson

She glanced up from the letter and saw that Garth was watching her. "This is pretty incredible. Do you suppose they're all like this?"

"Could be." His face was expressionless.

"I guess this is the up side. The down side was what happened today, with Eddie Gump. This is the reward part." Despite herself, she glowed with pride. She'd helped these people. Because of her book, their lives had been altered for the better.

Garth stood there fighting his emotions. Her eyes shone; her cheeks were flushed. The only other time he'd seen her look like that had been when he'd made love to her. If getting these letters made her this happy, they could be in big trouble. He swallowed and forced himself to ask the question, although he dreaded the answer. He gestured toward the pile of letters. "This is pretty powerful stuff, Kate. You're obviously idolized by your fans. Are you sure you still want to write that letter to Northbluff?"

15

KATE LOOKED into his eyes and wondered how much it had cost him to ask the question. "What if I said I didn't want to write the letter, that instead I wanted to keep on writing books?"

His expression grew bleak. "I—"

"You wouldn't feel the same about our future, would you?"

He shook his head.

"Neither would I." She stood, spilling letters out of her lap, and wrapped her arms around him. "We'll settle down in Northbluff, just as we planned. I haven't forgotten about Eddie Gump, and there could be others like him out there."

Garth sighed deeply and held her tight. "Of course there are. Writing another book and keeping yourself in the spotlight would be insane. You can take pride in what you've done, but one book is enough, Kate. They've had their piece of you. Let them find another guru to follow."

"Absolutely." Kate forced her mind away from the letters. Maybe she wouldn't even read the rest. Instead, she needed to think about returning to her classes and about buying a house in Northbluff—one big enough for a family. She needed to think about planting a garden in the spring, and spending her days and nights in quiet satisfaction and peace. She needed to think about the joy of loving Garth. "Let's get that letter written," she said, giving him one more squeeze.

KATE SAT in the green room of the television station and tried to concentrate on her breathing. If she could just relax, maybe she'd stop perspiring and maybe her hands wouldn't shake when she was on the set of *The Jerry Perry Show*.

At least she'd turned down all the offers that had come in after Eddie Gump was captured. All the prominent talk show hosts in the country were after her now, especially with her book on the *New York Times* bestseller list. Jerry Perry, when he'd come by the green room to see her earlier, had been bursting with smug pride that he was the only television personality with the "foresight," as he put it, to have signed her up before she became quite so famous. He implied that he'd read her book and "envisioned" a dynamite show with her as a guest.

Kate knew better. Glenda had known Jerry Perry since high school, which was how she'd wangled a spot for Kate on the show. Glenda had warned Kate that Jerry Perry never read anything more challenging than the comic page of the L.A. *Times*. Kate had tried to dissuade Glenda from approaching Perry, but Glenda had wanted her to do at least one nationally televised show. "One show won't kill you," Glenda had said. As Kate sat in the green room watching the second hand jerk around the white face of the clock, she wasn't so sure.

She almost wished now that she'd taken Garth up on his offer to come with her. But she'd thought about how much he disliked this sort of hoopla and had told him she'd see him in the suite afterward. This would be her last official act as "Dr. Kate," and then she could concentrate on becoming a professor, a wife, and if they were very lucky, a mother.

She'd talked to Donna again, and had learned that the faculty committee had been impressed with her faxed letter. Of course, the sensationalism surrounding the capture of Eddie Gump hadn't helped, and the *New York Times* list might as well have been a Ten Most Wanted list, Donna had said, for all the reaction it had caused. However, Donna was hopeful that Kate could keep her job.

Kate imagined that many of the faculty members would watch this program today before making their final decision. She knew exactly the impression she had to give, and she intended to give it. She'd left her hair styled the same way—she'd learned to like it—but she'd muted her makeup and chosen to wear flat shoes and a blouse and skirt in neutral colors. Jerry Perry had raised his eyebrows when he'd seen her. Kate had counted that as a good sign.

The first guest had already been called—a man with a trick chicken. The man, Neal Barnett, had seemed nice enough; while he'd been in the green room Kate had talked with him at length about his chicken—a special brown hen named Martha—to distract herself from the ordeal ahead. Neal and Martha would still be on the stage, she'd been told, when she was called. Kate tried to focus on that. One friend—two if she wanted to count Martha—would be out there with her. She'd count Martha.

She watched the clock until a young woman with a floral scarf artfully draped and pinned around her shoulders came into the green room. "Dr. Kate," the girl said, smiling with lips the color of red grapes, "Mr. Perry is about to announce you."

Adrenaline pumped through Kate, accelerating her heartbeat and dampening her palms as she followed the grape-lipped woman down a hall that felt as cold as a freezer compartment. She would never get used to this. Fortunately she didn't have to. This was it, her final performance as Dr. Kate. She thought of Garth. Garth would be watching. She'd focus on him to steady herself.

Silently the two women slipped inside a door. Kate heard the laughter of the studio audience and the clucking of a chicken. Then came the sound of flapping wings and applause.

"Well, Neal, you've trained that chicken so well, she'll make some man a good wife," Jerry Perry said.

Kate winced. This would be rougher than she'd thought.

"I'm anxious for you to meet our next guest," Perry continued. "She's in the business of training men, not chickens. Let's find out what tips we can learn from the bestselling author of *Getting the Sex You Need from Your Man*, the lovely Dr. Kate!"

No last name, even, Kate thought, fuming as she pasted a smile on her face and stepped through the opening in the curtain. She'd been warned not to squint at the sudden change to bright lights, but the effort to keep her eyes wide and her smile on was enormous. Applause—for her?—thundered in the small studio.

Jerry Perry, balding and round faced, rose from behind his desk and shook her hand. "Deceptive looking, isn't she, folks? Looks like a schoolteacher in that outfit, but let me tell you, this little lady knows the ropes about how to get guys to do all sorts of exciting things in bed. Right, Dr. Kate?"

Anger took hold of Kate, and for a moment she contemplated telling this grinning baboon exactly what she thought of him and his crackpot show. A couple of weeks ago she sure would have. Then she remembered Garth and his coolness under fire. She thought of all the speeches she'd given, the autographs she'd signed, and even the mugger she'd fought. She could handle this slimeball with one hand tied behind her back. She smiled. "I've learned to get men to do a lot of things," she said, "but I have trouble getting them to read my book. Tell me, Jerry, have you read it yet?"

The audience cheered. Jerry Perry faltered. He blushed. Finally he recovered himself, but not before Kate had scored a small victory.

"I'm an action man, myself," he said. "I'd rather do it than read about it."

The chicken squawked and the audience laughed. Kate knew they were more amused by the chicken than by the host of the show. She settled into her cushioned chair beside Perry's desk. She could do this.

Perry's questions were typical and many were filled with innuendo. Whenever Kate started to get angry, she glanced at the chicken. Martha always responded by cocking her head at Kate and staring back with one bright eye. Soon the audience noticed and began to titter.

"What's going on?" Perry asked her. "Are you actually communicating with that chicken?"

"Why not?" Kate responded. "She's had a lot of experience with cocky roosters, too." The audience applauded wildly. Kate had them completely on her side.

Finally Perry drew the segment to a close. "So what's next, Dr. Kate? Got a hot new bestseller in the works?"

"No." Kate had been hoping for the question. She looked straight into the camera, straight at Garth watching in their suite at the Pelican. "This is my first and last effort. I'm retiring from the book-writing business."

She was unprepared for the audience reaction. There was hushed silence, and then a murmur of protest that grew loud enough that Jerry Perry had to acknowledge it.

"It seems your fans aren't happy with that announcement, Dr. Kate."

For the first time since she'd walked onto the set she couldn't marshall her thoughts. "I'm . . . well, you see, I have another . . . there's—"

"And we're out of time!" Perry said, smiling his big-toothed grin at the camera. "I want to thank our two guests, Neal and his trick chicken Martha, and of course, Dr. Kate, the nation's current expert on getting the sex you need. See you all next week!"

The cameras clicked off but Kate remained in her chair, a little dazed.

A woman came forward and unclipped her microphone. "That's a shame, not writing another book. You've just gotten started. There's so much more to say!"

Kate glanced up at the female technician. She was right. After going through what she had in just the past two weeks, she had a lot more to tell people. And what about after she'd married Garth, after she'd had children, after she'd raised teenagers and faced menopause? She'd be able to help that many more people! But she'd promised the Northbluff faculty she was through. More important, she'd promised Garth. If she kept writing books, she'd lose her job, and she could very well lose Garth, too. He didn't want the limelight. She didn't want it, either, but could she stifle this need to communicate with other women? Hell, on the show she'd even tried to communicate with a female chicken!

Kate stood up and glanced around. Jerry Perry had left the set. His jovial character and love of people seemed to end when the taping did.

Neal was holding Martha in her cage. "Nice meeting you," he said to Kate. "I can understand why you'd want to give this up. Here come a mob of people after you. Want to make a run for it?"

Kate turned back toward the audience. With the camera lights off she could see the people better, and sure enough, a huge group was making its way toward the set. Kate knew she should take Neal's suggestion and run out the back. She could hop in the Pelican's van waiting outside the station and hightail it home to Garth before she did something stupid, something to ruin her entire future.

Then Kate made the mistake of looking at the chicken. Martha cocked an eye at Kate. "I'll stay," Kate said. "But you go ahead. Martha's been in that cage long enough."

"Yeah, she gets ornery if I keep her there," Neal said. "Well, good luck."

"Same to you." Then Kate turned and walked down the steps of the set and toward the crowd of women.

KATE PUT HER KEY in the lock and opened the door of the suite.

Garth stood just inside the door, his smile a mile wide. A bottle of champagne sat chilling on the table behind him. "You were terrific," he said, coming toward her. "And now it's over."

She put out her hand, stopping his progress. "No, it's not."

"What?"

Pain twisted in her heart. This could have been so easy. "It's not over, Garth. Before you kiss me, before you pop the cork on that champagne, you deserve to know what I've done. I've decided to write another book."

He stared at her, disbelief in his eyes. "But you said on TV that you were quitting. I heard you. Half the country heard you."

"I've come out of retirement." She was shaking, but the words sounded right. She didn't want to hurt him, but she couldn't hurt herself, either. Closing herself away in Northbluff would have been like trying to put the cork back in the champagne bottle once it was off.

"Why?" His question was an agonized moan.

"Because I have more to say. Because, ironically now that I've handled this tour and the talk show, I know I can do it again. I'll never love that part. I'll always be scared, but . . . Oh, Garth, don't you see? I have an ability to communicate, especially with women, and I can't turn my back on that. Women need to hear voices, comforting voices, right now, and I can be one of them. I'm good at it. I'm even growing fond of the name 'Dr. Kate.'"

His gaze remained steady. "You'll probably lose your job."

"I know. The fact is, I have a different job now. I'm a writer. I just wasn't willing to accept the change. Now I am."

"And I suppose you expect me to accept it, too?"

Her heart thundered. Here was the price she'd have to pay, and now that it loomed before her, she was less sure she could pay it. In order to be true to herself, she had to risk losing Garth. Yet it could be no other way. You couldn't save champagne; once you'd opened the bottle, you had to drink it all.

"I can't expect you to be happy with the choice I've made," she said, her voice trembling despite her resolve not to break down. "You're not bound to me in any way, Garth. You're free to seek a different path."

"You're wrong, Kate." He stepped forward. "I'm not free, and neither are you. We belong to each other, forever."

Kate thought of Martha in the cage. "Garth, you don't understand. I have to keep writing. It's the only choice for me."

"And I have to keep loving you. It's the only choice for me."

"But how—"

"I don't know just yet." He gathered her close. "But if you're going to be a bestselling author, then it looks like I'll be the husband of a bestselling author."

She gazed up at him, not quite believing what she was hearing. "But you said you wanted a quiet life, in a small town like Northbluff."

"I want you more. I love you, Kate. That's all that matters. We'll find another small town where we can hide when the going gets rough. Authors do it all the time." He smiled. "That'll be my department. I kind of like the idea of the challenge."

"Oh, Garth." Her eyes filled with tears. "I love you so much. This next book will be all about you."

"With the names changed to protect the innocent, I hope?"

"Of course." She caressed his cheek. "But, Garth, there are so many things I want to say. I want to talk to women about what it's like to be a mother, and—"

"A mother?" He grinned and pulled her closer. "I wondered if that idea had gone out the window with the professorship."

"Not if you're still willing to be the father, it hasn't."

"I'm not only willing, I'm intensely able." He leaned down and kissed her thoroughly. "In fact, I think the champagne can wait, don't you?"

"There are many ways to celebrate," she murmured, running her tongue over his lips.

"And I know them all," he said, scooping her up in his arms. "After all, I've read your book, Dr. Kate."

GLEANED FROM THE TABLOIDS:

Dr. Kate Gives Birth!

At an undisclosed hospital in northern California, famed sex expert Kate Newberry gave birth to a baby girl today. Sources say her husband, renowned financier Garth Fredericks, was at her side. A mere nine months ago the couple was wed in a much-publicized but well-guarded ceremony in the wine country north of San Francisco. The ceremony was quiet except for helicopters circling over the inn and at least one reporter who disguised himself as a deer and invaded the lawn party reception held after the ceremony. The security team hired by Fredericks threw the deer out but not before he had snapped the following photo of a very irate Fredericks hurling a champagne bottle at the camera.

Dr. Kate's Stalker Gets Feminist Shrink!

Famed celebrity stalker Eddie Gump, who terrorized Dr. Kate Newberry last year, is currently undergoing treatment at a mental hospital in Houston. His psychiatrist, Dr. Carolyn Biggers, is reputed to be a generous contributor to the National Organization for Women.

Faculty Glad They Dumped Dr. Kate!

Members of the Northbluff College faculty in Northbluff, Nebraska, have expressed relief that they canceled the contract of Dr. Kate Newberry last year. "We would have been overrun with undesirable types here at Northbluff," said an anonymous professor. Another anonymous source reported an interesting phenomenon in the town, however. She said the sale of tabloid newspapers has jumped astronomically in the past few months.

Dr. Kate's Agent Deluged
With Authors Begging
'Make Me Another Dr. Kate'!

Literary agent Glenda Detmeyer reports that she can barely see over her desk due to piles of unread manuscripts. She takes on very few new clients these days, she said, due to the record-breaking publisher's offer for Dr. Kate's latest manuscript. "The book, titled *Getting the Sex You Need After Childbirth*, requires a little more research before it can be completed and released," Detmeyer said. Which tells this reporter that financier Garth Fredericks will be a busy man during the next few weeks.

HARLEQUIN®

Temptation®

Rebels & Rogues

Trey: He lived life on the edge . . . and wasn't about to be
tamed by a beautiful woman.

THE RED-BLOODED YANKEE!
By Ruth Jean Dale
Temptation #413, October

All men are not created equal. Some are rough around the
edges. Tough-minded but tenderhearted. Incredibly
sexy. The tempting fulfillment of every woman't fantasy.

When it's time to fight for what they believe in, to win
that special woman, our Rebels and Rogues are heroes at
heart. Twelve Rebels and Rogues, each month in 1992,
only from Harlequin Temptation. Don't miss the
upcoming books by our fabulous authors such as Janice
Kaiser and Kelly Street.

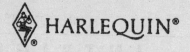

THE TAGGARTS OF TEXAS!

Harlequin's Ruth Jean Dale brings you
THE TAGGARTS OF TEXAS!

Those Taggart men—strong, sexy and hard to resist...

You've met Jesse James Taggart in FIREWORKS!
Harlequin Romance #3205 (July 1992)

Now meet Trey Smith—he's THE RED-BLOODED YANKEE!
Harlequin Temptation #413 (October 1992)

Then there's Daniel Boone Taggart in SHOWDOWN!
Harlequin Romance #3242 (January 1993)

And finally the Taggarts who started it all—in LEGEND!
Harlequin Historical #168 (April 1993)

Read all the Taggart romances!
Meet all the Taggart men!

Available wherever Harlequin books are sold.

A SPAULDING AND DARIEN MYSTERY

Amateur sleuths Jenny Spaulding and Peter Darien have set the date for their wedding. But before they walk down the aisle, love must pass a final test. This time, they won't have to solve a murder, they'll have to prevent one—Jenny's. Don't miss the chilling conclusion to the SPAULDING AND DARIEN MYSTERY series in October. Watch for:

#197 WHEN SHE WAS BAD by Robin Francis

Look for the identifying series flash—A SPAULDING AND DARIEN MYSTERY—and join Jenny and Peter for danger and romance....

WELCOME TO

The quintessential small town, where everyone
knows everybody else!

Finally, books that capture the pleasure
of tuning in to your favorite TV show!

Join your friends at Tyler in the eighth book, BACHELOR'S PUZZLE by Ginger
Chambers, available in October.

*What do Tyler's librarian and a cosmopolitan architect have in common? What
does the coroner's office have to reveal?*

GREAT READING...GREAT SAVINGS...
AND A FABULOUS FREE GIFT!

Each book set in Tyler is a self-contained love story; together, the twelve novels
stitch the fabric of the community. You can't miss the Tyler books on the shelves
because the covers honor the old American tradition of quilting; each cover
depicts a patch of the large Tyler quilt!

And you can receive a FABULOUS GIFT, ABSOLUTELY FREE, by collecting
proofs-of-purchase found in each Tyler book, *and* use our Tyler coupons to save
on your next TYLER book purchase.

HARLEQUIN®

Temptation®

the Fortune Boys

A funny, sexy miniseries from bestselling
author Elise Title!

**LOSING THEIR HEARTS MEANT
LOSING THEIR FORTUNES...**
If any of the four Fortune brothers were unfortunate
enough to wed, they'd be permanently divorced from
the Fortune millions—thanks to their father's last will
and testament.

**BUT CUPID HAD OTHER PLANS FOR
DENVER'S MOST ELIGIBLE BACHELORS!**
Meet Adam in #412 **ADAM & EVE** (Sept. 1992)
Meet Peter in #416 **FOR THE LOVE OF PETE**
   (Oct. 1992)
Meet Truman in #420 **TRUE LOVE** (Nov. 1992)
Meet Taylor in #424 **TAYLOR MADE** (Dec. 1992)

**WATCH THESE FOUR MEN TRY TO WIN AT
LOVE AND NOT FORFEIT $$$**